D0061643

Birds On A Wire Media
120 Marketplace Circle
Suite C #362
Georgetown, KY 40324
www.birdsonawiremedia.com

For information for speaking events or interviews with the author go to:
georgiacurtisling.com

For Phil, my keeper of promises.

Contents

SANTA'S Promising CHRISTMAS

georgia curtis ling

A Spring Valley Heartwarming Romance
BOOK TWO

BIRDS ON A WIRE MEDIA

For He who promised is faithful.

SANTA'S PROMISING CHRISTMAS

BY

GEORGIA CURTIS LING

©2022

Chapter One

His remorseful grief always weighed heavier on his heart this time of year. After twenty years, Rich thought it would diminish. There were days it never entered his mind—those were few and far between. The holidays were such a contradiction for him. They were filled with joy and celebration. Yet, it also carried melancholy that invariably unearthed regrets.

Rich Ramsey sat alone at a booth, tucked back in a corner of the Mockingbird Coffee House, sipping his coffee. Alone with his memories—his secrets. Only a handful of people in Spring Valley knew that almost twenty years ago, Rich stepped out of denial into God's grace and began his recovery journey. Rich was a drunk that allowed his habits and hang-ups to destroy his family. A tragedy brought him face-to-face with reality, and he humbly began his road to recovery. Sometimes, it was a lonely road. Rich constantly reminded himself that he's not alone with God by his side. A scripture promise came to his mind: *He heals the brokenhearted and binds up their wounds.* His heart was felt lighter.

"If I didn't know better, from the look on your face, I would think you were the loneliest man in town." Ada Taylor interrupted his thoughts, as she topped off his coffee.

The aroma of the fresh brew continued to improve his mood.

Rich managed a smile, thinking to himself, *if she only knew.* "Good morning, Ada! Don't worry about me, I'm just lost in thought." Rich stirred his sweetener and cream in his coffee. "I always feel like I've been to church when I stop in here. It has a way of setting my heart and mind in a good place. You should have named it Holy Grounds." Rich knew it was a corny thing to say, but he laughed at his own joke. He diverted his attention. "I think its miraculous that the one hundred-and fifty-year-old stained-glass windows are still intact. When the sunlight scatters all the colors, it gives off a spiritual vibe."

Ada glanced around and admired the historic church building. "The windows and the vaulted ceiling were two of the reasons I fell in love with this place. When I retired from teaching, J.R. thought I would just enjoy being *First Lady* at AME Zion Church, but I had the tug of a divine calling. I can remember the exact moment I knew this was for me. When I walked through those doors with the realtor, something deep inside stirred my heart and soul. That very day, I stepped out in faith, purchased this old church, and started my coffee house."

"Well, I can testify that it was a divine calling because your desserts are divine." Rich couldn't believe another cliché comment rolled off his tongue. He tried to save himself from total embarrassment. "I'm sure you've heard that one before."

"I love hearing that over and over!" Ada was proud of her decadent confections. "J.R. ministers to his parishioners. I take care of my coffee house patrons."

Rich pointed to the sign posted over the door that read, *The Lord bless thee, and keep thee.* "Was that plaque here when you bought the building?"

"No, I added that scripture blessing. Just in case I don't get a chance to say *God bless you* to my customers as they exit; I want that to be the last thing they see as they head out for the rest of their day." Ada loved talking about her sanctuary. "I just want people to feel blessed when they walk in and out of that door."

Rich admired Ada for her expression of faith. She was truly a town treasure.

Ada shifted the subject. "Isn't it a little early for you to be showing up in town? The pumpkin farm just wrapped up their fall festival last weekend." Ada rattled on_as she had the tendency to do. "Fortunately, no child got lost in their giant corn maze. Just the thought of it makes me anxious." A lot of things made Ada anxious. "If

I'm not mistaken, the first Santa event isn't until after Thanksgiving." Ada had a little extra time, so she scooted in to the booth across from Rich for a quick little chat.

"Well, that's a fine how-do-you-do! Am I only allowed in town when I'm donning the red suit?" Rich loved teasing Ada.

"You know that's not what I meant. It's always great to see you in street clothes or your Santa costume. By the way," Ada leaned in closer and whispered, "with your fit physique, no one would ever guess you're jolly old Saint Nick."

"Why, Ada, if I didn't know better I would think you were flirting with me." Rich flashed that million-dollar smile. "Does J.R. know you hit on your customers?"

She winked and laughed. "If it gets me a better tip, he won't mind." After forty-two anniversaries, her love for J.R. had never waned. Her husband had nothing to worry about.

"I admit, the fat suit padding transforms me with that big jolly belly." Rich sipped his coffee. "A lot of my fellow professional Santas go for the full natural look. Nothing is fake, but a big belly is where I draw the line." Rich did what had to be done to keep his toned body. He ran and lifted weights. He did pull-ups, push-ups, burpees, biked, hiked_anything he enjoyed to keep his fifty-eight-year-old body and mind healthy and in shape. He was open to whatever helped keep him on his recovery journey.

Steering the conversation back to Ada's original question, Rich replied, "I'm in town to meet with Spring Valley's holiday event coordinator to nail down my appearances. Since we practically skipped Christmas last year, due to the shutdown, the demand for Santa is at an all-time high." Rich's smile faded remembering the sad year, as he stirred another packet of sweetener in his coffee. "Since my calendar will be booked solid, after I finish my breakfast, I'm walking over to the Spring Valley Inn to see if I can reserve a room for two or three weeks, so I don't spend all my time driving back and forth to my house out in the country."

With the mention of the inn, Ada's favorite hobby of matchmaking kicked into high gear. "You'll love the new owners, especially Alana. I think you two might hit it off." She tried to conceal her giddiness, but failed miserably.

Rich shook his head and smiled. "You never give up, do you, Ada?"

Ada teasingly wagged her finger at Rich. "You've got admit, I did pretty good with Gabe and Shauna. Their wedding bells will be ringing in a few weeks."

"I don't think wedding bells are in my near future." Rich secretly questioned if he even deserved a second chance at love. "I hear Gabe and Shauna asked if you would officiate their wedding."

"Yes! I'm so excited. It will be my first."

Ada's eyes twinkled. "It's such a great honor. I was thrilled when they wanted to hold their wedding here at the Mockingbird, and then when they asked if I would perform the ceremony, that was just icing on the wedding cake!" Ada giggled at her own joke and patted the table top. "Gabe and Shauna's love story began in this very booth when they were paired up as teammates to sponsor a wishing ornament from the Giving Tree." Her face beamed with pride. "I just knew those two were meant for each other. This coffee house has proven to be a place of new beginnings."

Rich thought he could definitely use a new beginning.

***

As he stepped outside the warmth of the coffee house, the crisp fall air invigorated him. Rich loved this time of year. He had traveled all over, but by far he thought fall foliage in the Appalachian Mountains was one of the most breathtaking, unbelievable views he had ever seen. He felt as if he were an eyewitness to God's paint pallet as the mountains transformed from deep dark hues of green to gorgeous fall colors with brilliant shades of red, yellow, and orange. It impressed him that the little town went all out for the changing seasons because they knew that tourism helped the local artisans survive. Rich always enjoyed walking the brick paved sidewalks in this little historic town. Main Street was decorated with tall, dried corn shucks tied around the lamp posts with bailing twine, surrounded at the base with vibrant red, purple, and yellow chrysanthemums. Nature astounded him. Just the thought that when trees needed to reserve energy to survive, wind gust gave aid with that final push to say goodbye to their leaves. As they slowly floated to the ground around Rich's feet, it resembled a colorful patchwork quilt, like his granny once crafted in days gone by. That memory brought a smile to his face. Leaves crunched underneath his footsteps. The earthy smells of fall hung in the air. Rich knew Tennessee weather was fickle. In a few weeks, the vibrant colors would fade, replaced with a dull, gray winter that would trail close behind. The sidewalks would soon be covered with a blanket of snow, and local shop owners would diligently shovel a path for their much-needed Christmas shoppers.

It was a quick walk to the inn and only a few short blocks to the town hall where he would meet the town event coordinator. He would stop in for a quick reservation inquiry and be on his way.

He walked alone, as he did most days. With no one to balance the conversation, his mind took a familiar path as he strolled along. *Why don't I just give up on my Christmas wish?* Rich lamented. For the past two decades, it had been the same wish year-after-year.

The last time he saw his daughter, Courtney, it was on her eighteen birthday—the day she became an adult in the eyes of the law. She swore she would never again step foot in his house. So far, she'd kept her word. It broke his heart. Throughout his career he'd kept the same phone number. Once, maybe twice a year, she would text using a private number, careful not to reveal her whereabouts. At least the welcomed text messages let him know she was still alive. He sold the house a few years after she stormed out the front door. He didn't know where she lived. He didn't know if she was married. He didn't know if he had grandkids. He didn't know much of anything.

Courtney didn't know her dad was a changed man. She didn't know that his personal recovery journey began two years after she stepped off the front porch and walked away because that's when he stepped out of his own denial and walked into God's grace. Rich thought if she only could see the man he'd become—the new man—she'd realize he'd truly changed. He only had one Christmas wish—that their paths would cross, and he would be given a second chance. He realized she would be a grown woman now; he was well aware appearance drastically changes in twenty years, he thought to himself. He was afraid he wouldn't even recognize his own flesh and blood. He hoped and prayed if they ever had a divine encounter, something about him would be familiar, and she would know her own dad. But if he were honest with himself, and he tried to be, he had doubts.

Every morning he recited the *Serenity*

Prayer, reminding himself to accept the things he cannot change and asking for courage to change the things he could. He prayed without ceasing that one day his daughter's heart would soften.

Some days his mind betrayed him and drove his thoughts to the dark land of hopelessness. It was a daily contest of strength. There were days he wanted to drown away those thoughts. Numb the pain. Rich knew he could only take one day at a time. After all, he thought—that's all any of us had.

One of the things Rich took away from the world of his NASCAR days as a crew chief was knowing when adversity strikes, you had to remain cool and calm. He was well aware that at the end of the race, the strategy he implemented with his crew in each pit stop would make him a winner or loser for his team. Most days, his tried-and-true strategies worked against his own mind games, as a glimmer of hope would flicker, illuminate his dark thoughts, and drive him safely out of the land of hopelessness. Rich was determined that today was definitely going to be one of those hope days. Hope would take the lead, one thought at a time, and pull him into a victory lane. Maybe this would be the year when everything he wished for came true—a Christmas of forgiveness and a family reunion.

Chapter Two

Alana sat staring at her computer screen, viewing the online reservations, wondering if her risk-taking had led her and her sister, Jean, down a bankruptcy path. The last year and a half were not what she'd envisioned for the business venture she and Jean plunged in to headfirst.

Alana reflected on how she was first introduced to Spring Valley several years ago when her nephew, Gabe, had moved to Spring Valley with his new bride to manage her family's historic inn. She never imagined that in a few short years, her nephew would be a widower, running the inn alone in Spring Valley. Alana's heart ached for Gabe as she watched months turn to years as he journeyed on his own. In the course of time, she was thrilled when Gabe found love and a new beginning when he met Shauna Murphy, who came home for the holidays to spend with her family. During their holiday romance, Gabe decided he would no longer live in the past. He wanted a future with Shauna.

Alana knew firsthand that dreams change. People change. Before a new love entered Gabe's life, he'd asked his mom, Jean, if she would help him run the inn. That's when Alana entered the picture. Jean decided she didn't want to work for her son; instead, she and his Aunt Alana wanted to buy the inn. Not manage. Own. After many sister-to-sister conversations, they decided that Alana's years of experience from working at the Inn at the Biltmore Estate in Asheville, combined with Jean's expertise as a chef, were the perfect ingredients for a recipe for success. A small inn, a small town, a big adventure for two sisters in semi-retirement. Plus, it would free Gabe to start a new life with Shauna and pursue his own interests. Gabe decided he wasn't abandoning his deceased wife's legacy. She wouldn't be betrayed because she would have been proud. He was confident his mother and aunt would carry on her vision.

Alana knew.

She knew it would work. She was the architect of their business plan. She received a Hotel Restaurant Institutional Management Degree from Boston University. After college, she was hired at the prestigious XV Beacon in Boston, eventually retaining the post of front office manager. After moving to Asheville, North Carolina, over sixteen years ago with her surgeon husband, Daniel Davis, she took the only available position at the Inn on the Biltmore Estate as a guest experience host, then the historian, and ultimately, promoted to the front office manager.

She knew she could run a small, boutique,

twelve-room inn with her eyes closed. She knew she would love working side-by side with her sister—her forever best friend.

Although raised in the same home together, they were as different as night and day. Where Alana was ivory, fair-skinned, Jean was olive-brown. Alana was petite; Jean was tall and full-figured. Both were attractive. Even though she was younger, Jean was the stable and wise mother hen; Alana was the easy-going adventurer. Alana knew that sometimes Jean envied Alana's venturesome spirit, but stability was required in parenthood, especially since Jean raised Gabe as a single mom. Though poles apart in features and personalities, their life-long friendship was bound by an enduring sister-love.

After fourteen years of marriage, Alana's husband chose another. Divorce followed. Subsequently, she dated Everett Davenport on and off for years. Everett ended up being an uncommittable guy. Alana was more of a commitment-type-of-gal and ended that relationship. She loved her position at the Biltmore, but Alana knew she was ready for a new beginning.

Alana was surprised when she broached the subject of semi-retiring and buying the inn from Gabe, and without hesitation, Jean agreed and said she was ready for a new adventure. Alana and Jean tapped into their own retirement funds to finance the purchase. Within weeks, they were the proud new owners of Spring Valley Inn. She knew it would be a success.

What she didn't know—a contagion outbreak, on the other side of the world, would spread to their small mountain town and shutter their inn last year.

She knew they needed a Christmas miracle.

The vintage shopkeeper's doorbell alerted Alana of someone's entry to the inn. The whimsical, brass decorative owl, perched on a branch that held the bell, had been a fixture at the inn for almost two centuries. It even survived three fires. Nearly all of their guests commented on the period charm of the bell. It especially fit in perfectly during the Christmas holiday, and without exception, every day someone would say, "Every time a bell rings, an angel gets its wings." It took a couple of months for Alana to adjust to the sound, but the quaint tone became a pleasant, gentle greeting.

"Hello! I'm Alana. Welcome to Spring Valley Inn. How may I assist you?" She greeted the visitor with a smile. He looked perfect, she thought. Alana wished she had touched up her lipstick after the last cup of coffee. He had a presence that immediately drew her in. His eyes—very kind, smoky gray eyes—and his salt and pepper gray hair were an alluring combination. She admired a man who didn't feel the need to invest in *Just For Men* and wash away the gray. The silver fox look worked for him. Alana stared as Rich walked across the room in her direction.

His mouth curved in response to her pleasant greeting. After more than a year of social distancing, he could barely remember the last time he shook someone's hand. Touch mattered. He missed that physical contact for human connection. It was part of his DNA. Today, seeing the woman behind the desk, he missed it now—more than ever.

Rich noticed her unadorned finger on her left hand. He wondered if a band of gold had ever filled the void. His personal thoughts shouldn't come as a surprise. After all, only a few minutes ago, Ada had laid the matchmaking groundwork. But Ada didn't reveal any backstory. He decided he would have to do a little investigating on his own.

The charming antiques that filled the room caught his eye. There was an ornate fireplace that held a glowing flame directly behind the half circle rich mahogany executive desk. Rich thought it was a work of furniture art, a dramatic focal point for the parlor and the beautiful woman who was seated behind the rare desk. On the surface sat a small laptop, a blend of past and present. The right wall held historic photographs of the inn, dated back two hundred years. A testament of the significance the historic inn held in Spring Valley.

At first glance, the woman reminded Rich more of a big-city trend setter than a small-town innkeeper. Her unconventional, free-spirited, Bohemian style leaned strongly toward the hippie fashion of his youth. He'd read somewhere that it's now referred to as *boho fashion*. Whatever it's called, he liked it.

Her intoxicating green eyes held a hint of nature, the hue of the mountains in the summertime. The warm sunrays of autumn shown through the front windows falling on her wisps of stunning silver that wove through her hair. Maybe her short, sassy cut held a clue to her personality. To him, embracing her natural color and a slight messiness read fun and carefree. He wondered if the soft lines in her face were a testament to a happy life, full of joyful facial expressions, or did those lines hold hints of worry and sadness? He was betting on joyful. Alana stood and motioned for him to take a seat across from her desk.

"I'm Rich Ramsey." He casually introduced himself. "I'll be in town on business two, possibly three weeks after Thanksgiving," he continued, "I was hoping you might have a room available." Rich deeply inhaled the sweet aromas wafting from the kitchen. "I'm also hoping whatever I'm smelling will be served every day."

"You can count on it!" Alana smiled in agreement. "Chef Jean, the co-owner of the inn, is also an award-winning chef and culinary instructor. I guarantee dining here will never be a disappointment."

Alana didn't have to check her computer reservations system; she knew there was availability. She had hoped there would be no room at the inn this Christmas, but hopes and wishes didn't pay the bills. Alana was desperately trying to keep the inn from being a casualty of the pandemic shutdown. In the inn's full fight for survival, she and Jean used additional funds in their dwindling nest egg which became their piggy bank to finance ongoing operational needs. She reminded herself that they were fortunate. Many of the small inns permanently closed. As the world slowly opened, the following spring brought renewal with a few tourists, summer brought loyal NASCAR fans, and she hoped Christmas would provide the much-needed financial boost.

She didn't want to look desperate, so she tapped away on the keyboard, stared at the computer screen for a moment, looked up and shared the good news. "It looks like we have the Maxwell room available. It's a nice, over-sized room on our second level, with access to the porch overlooking Main Street, where this time of year visitors have a prime location to watch holiday parades. It's one of our most requested rooms. With tax included the nightly rate will be $299.00. " She smiled, crossed her fingers in her mind, and waited for his response.

"Yes, that's perfect. Let's book November twenty-fourth through December fifteenth." Rich reached into his back pocket for his wallet, pulled out a credit card, and handed it to Alana to guarantee the reservation.

Alana went into full hotel mode as she inserted the credit card into the Square Terminal. "All of our accommodations offer spacious, quiet rooms with private baths, free WI-FI, satellite television, central heat and air with individual controls, acoustic soundproofing, in-room safes, and all natural bath products." She continued without missing a beat, "We have a 48-hours' cancellation window, with no fee. If you cancel later, you'll be responsible for a one night's stay."

"No need to worry, I'll be here with bells on." Rich grinned. Little did she know, he thought, he would literally have bells stashed away in his suitcase along with his red suit.

Rich made small talk as she finished the transaction. He actually regretted that he needed to head to an appointment with the town's event coordinator, but he really didn't want to be late.

"Alana, thank you. It was nice meeting you. I'll see you in a few weeks." He stood to leave.

Curious, Alana wondered what line of work he was in that would require him to be in Spring Valley over the holiday. Usually, this time of year, the inn was filled with out-of-town guests visiting relatives or tourists attending the Appalachian Christmas Heritage Festival. Rich didn't offer an explanation, and she chose not to inquire.

Alana stood behind the desk. Her eyes gleamed. "It was my pleasure; I'm looking forward to your stay."

As soon as she heard her own words, she

thought they may have possessed a flirtatious tint. She should have said, *we're looking forward to your stay*. When his smile broadened, it confirmed her own suspicion. Her sister always accused her of being a flirt. This time she may have been right. Alana thought about rephrasing her reply but feared she would only dig a deeper hole. Truth be told, she was looking forward to getting to know this mysterious stranger.

Rich bid Alana farewell. As he opened the door, the whimsical bell rang. He turned for one last glimpse of Alana and smiled. He thought there might just be a promising Christmas in store for him after all.

Chapter Three

Alana could hardly contain her excitement. She popped in the kitchen to share the news with Jean. The room was cozy and smelled like the scent of Christmas, a delicious blend of creamy vanilla bean with hints of nutmeg, cinnamon, and brown sugar. Jean finished piping the icing on the cookies and munched on a gingerbread man's arm, while standing at the kitchen island with her eyes fixed on the giant whiteboard wall calendar. She was in her traditional, professional chef's uniform of hat, white double-breasted jacket with knotted cloth buttons and embroidered name, loose-fitting pants in a black and white houndstooth pattern, and classic black clogs. Alana knew that her sister was well aware that her derriere should never wear any form of checkered patterns, but Jean chose to wear it to honor the history and respect of her chosen profession. Alana was just thankful Jean didn't wear those modern crazy printed pants. Alana could handle the houndstooth, but she threatened to wrestle her sister to the ground if she ever stepped foot out of the kitchen in those wild pants.

"I have great news!" Alana reached for a cookie, but remembering her commitment to cut out sweets, she drew her hand back as if she touched a hot stove. Jean didn't notice as she stood zombie-like staring at the wall. "Hello!" Alana patted Jean's shoulder, "Are you in there?"

Jean turned toward Alana and nonchalantly chose another cookie. "I'm sorry, I'm working on the schedule for the holiday. It's great that we're getting busy, but the Christmas season is a non-stop chain of holiday happenings beginning with Gabe and Shauna's wedding rehearsal dinner, private dinner parties, and the pop-up cookie decorating shop. Plus, that's not including our regular guests' continental breakfast, snacks, and dinner." Jean puffed a blast of air through her lips and took another bite of her cookie. "Just trying to fit everything in. What are you all excited about?"

"I just booked a twenty-one-night length of stay!" Alana was bursting with joy. "I'm beginning to love the holidays!"

"That's fantastic!" Jean's eyes widened. "That should definitely help our occupancy rate."

"Absolutely, each month it climbs." Alana, did some quick math in her head. "We're up to 38% occupancy, which is an average of four rooms per night." Alana was cautiously optimistic, but felt a dash of hope. "With the holidays, reservations are picking up. Out-of-town guests are visiting relatives, and families are driving in for the Appalachian Christmas Festival this month."

"Before we bought the inn and the pandemic shut us down, Gabe had an 80% occupancy rate. It's taken a long time, but Sis, we're crawling out, day by day! Hopefully, with more rooms booked, a successful pop-up Christmas cookie shop, and the private parties, we'll have a profitable December." In celebration, Jean clapped her hands. "Who booked the room for so long, especially during the holiday?"

"He's a bit of a mystery man. Very intriguing, though."

"Don't hold back." Eyebrows lifted, Jean inquired. "Tell me more."

"He didn't overshare, and I didn't probe. All he said was he was here on business."

"So, it's not a family trip." Jean surmised. "Did you notice if he wore a wedding band?"

"I did notice. He didn't. He's also a silver fox, very handsome, hip, and had a Matthew McConaughey twang, that mumbly speaking style. I kept waiting for him to say, 'alright, alright, alright.'" Alana had Jean's attention.

"Interesting." Jean poured another cup of coffee, grabbed the plate of cookies, pulled out a chair at the table stationed beside the warmth of the cozy fireplace, and settled down for a sister-to-sister chat. She offered Alana a cookie.

"Isn't it a little early for Christmas cookies? We just celebrated Halloween."

"I made a batch to try out my new gingerbread recipe for the pop-up cookie shop.

Taste one and tell me what you think."

"You'll have to wait until Craig comes on shift." Alana patted her waist. "I'm swearing off sugar."

"I admire your self-restraint, but this is a ridiculous time to say no to sweets. There's temptation around every corner." Jean grinned and took a bite of the rejected cookie. "Good luck with that."

Coffee in hand, Alana took her lead, sat down relaxed across the table from Jean and began discussing the same topic spoken over and over since they had been children, except it expanded from boys to men.

"His name is Rich Ramsey, with emphasis on the 'Rich' because he held the reservation with a black American Express card, like the one Father would let us use from time-to-time." Alana saw the premium luxury credit card frequently at the Inn on the Biltmore Estate, but it was an unexpected, high-end card to see in Spring Valley.

"That name sounds familiar." Jean pulled out her phone and scrolled for an email. "Found it! He's on Gabe and Shauna's rehearsal dinner invitation list."

"He didn't mention that he would be in town for the dinner. I wonder how he's connected."

Alana and Jean had lived in Spring Valley for almost two years, but with social distancing from the world, they hadn't had the opportunity to get to know too many people.

Jean looked at the clock on the wall which brought her back to reality. "I would love to chat longer, but I have a full day ahead. I've got to get back to this calendar." She picked up a marker to fill in some dates. "I just have one more question. Is he your type?"

Alana walked to the sink to rinse her coffee mug. "I have a type?"

With a laugh, Jean teased her younger sister, "You know you do. Everybody has a type. The top description on your list is mysterious." She smirked. "Evidently, Rich has Shauna's families' stamp of approval since he's on their rehearsal dinner guest list. I think this one may be worth investigating." Jean added, turning to Alana, "I also think you're up for a magical holiday romance."

She'd have to agree that her sister had a point. Rich was definitely mysterious. Alana's social life was on a temporary hiatus. At her present juncture in life, she supposed she was interested enough. In the few short minutes of their encounter, he'd definitely piqued her curiosity. She had to admit she had romantic thoughts. Thoughts, Alana reminded herself, she shouldn't possess about guests.

Chapter Four

The Appalachian Heritage Woodworking shop was Rich's last scheduled stop in Spring Valley. Rich loved how this town celebrated its mountain roots and was proud that his life-long, best friend, Ryan Murphy, was a huge part of the town's success. Ryan, an internationally known Appalachian artisan, literally carved out a living building custom designed exquisite furniture, a mountain tradition of building furniture passed on from generation to generation.

Rich was a proud owner of several of Ryan's meticulous, one-of-a-kind masterpieces. One design, in particular, he thought, would be the envy of anyone who ever donned a red suit and played Father Christmas. On a whim, Rich commissioned Ryan to build a custom, cherry wood, Santa-themed coffin adorned with carved Christmas images of trees, ornaments, and toys on the side and a carved Santa sleigh on the lid. The lining was red satin, trimmed with white fur. Upon completion, after the private unveiling, though stunning and far more than Rich had imagined, Rich regretted not putting more thought into his impulsive request. Standing beside his funerary box, he faced the reality of death. A certainty he hoped was far, far away in the distant future. Rich reflected on years ago when he'd owned up to his failings, consciously relinquished control of his life, and placed God in the driver's seat to protect and guide his decisions, but Rich still had relationships he needed to mend before he left this earth.

The coffin was relocated from the workshop to Rich's home media room. It was an interesting conversation piece; however, the daily sight of the casket gave him a sense of urgency to make amends.

The wood shop smelled of forest. Rich walked into a haze of sawdust particles and the buzzing sound of saws and sanders, mixed in with the music. Legendary Marty Stuart's rock 'n' roll twang signature sound blared loud enough to be heard over the noise cancellation headsets each employee wore. They reminded him of the racing headphones for NASCAR scanners. Instead of listening to music, fans listened to their favorite drivers, pit crews, and commentators at the track on race day, all the while protecting their hearing. Rich wished he had a pair in the truck. Ryan turned off his saw, looked up, and saw Rich pinching his nose, attempting to halt a sneeze. Ryan stood, dusted off his pants, and walked over to greet Rich with a bear hug. Ryan motioned Rich to his private office. Rich waved at the work crew as he passed their crowded work areas.

"This is an unexpected visit." Ryan closed the office door, shutting out the noise.

"I was in the neighborhood, meeting with the event coordinator to nail down my Santa appearances. I thought I would stop in to say hello and check on the chair."

Ryan knew what chair he meant. After Rich attended Santa Claus school, Ryan built him a tall, wooden, high back throne chair, decorated with elves, toys, a Santa engraving carved in the wood, and green velvet upholstery. The chair was the spark that led to the artful coffin conception. It was a magical, fairytale design, fit for a king, but made for one of the most famous people in the world. Ryan was proud of the throne he handcrafted and how it made him feel part of a sweet, everlasting memory in a child's mind.

"It's not in the workshop," Ryan disclosed. "Since you didn't use it last year, I moved it to storage in Colleen's Christmas shop with the rest of the decorations and props for Santa's Train Depot."

"That's no problem," Ryan assured him. He trusted Colleen would guard it with her life. He had been best man at Ryan and Colleen's wedding over three decades ago. Rich valued her friendship; she was a good confidante. She always made him feel like part of the family. "You don't have to worry about setting it up. The events coordinator just needed to know where to locate the chair."

"I'll give her a call later today and let her

know where her crew can pick it up," Ryan said. "By the way, I haven't seen the RSVP list for Gabe and Shauna's rehearsal dinner, but I'm assuming you'll be there." He paused for a moment and added, "You know it will break Shauna's heart if you're a no-show."

"Wild horses couldn't keep me away." Rich was an unofficial uncle to Ryan's girls.

"I'm sure it will be chaotic, but you are welcome to stay at our house, or we can book you a night at Spring Valley Inn. It would be convenient; Gabe's mom is hosting the event." Ryan had an ulterior motive to suggest lodging at the inn.

Rich saw the mischievous smile that Ryan couldn't conceal.

"I know what you're up to, old friend." Rich had grown accustomed to Ryan trying to fix him up. "Ada beat you to it this morning, playing matchmaker."

Ryan's grin spread wide. "Just trying to help a friend in need."

"What makes you think I'm in need?" Ryan protested.

"Do you want me to make a list? It's a long one." Ryan sat down at his desk, picked up his scratch pad, reached for his pencil, and started writing. "I'll write them in your own words."

Ryan read the list out loud as he wrote.

I'm too busy, I don't have time to date around.
I failed at love one too many times.
I don't have any luck meeting women my own

age.

I don't want something just casual.

Second chances are a myth.

"Okay, okay. You can stop." Rich threw his hands up in surrender and plopped in the chair across from the desk.

"Since Gabe sold the inn to his mom and aunt, Colleen and I have spent a lot of time with them, and we both agree that Alana would be a great match for you. You don't have to live alone, you know."

Over the years, Ryan was guilty of pushing women on his best friend. Sometimes, he knew down deep it wouldn't last, but he also knew his friend lived a lonely life. It was risky to play matchmaker with Alana and Rich. If it didn't work, it would make for awkward social gatherings. Ryan truly felt they would be a good match and decided it could be worth a shot.

When Ryan looked up from the list and saw Rich's clenched jaw and furrowed brow, he thought, *maybe not.*

Rich didn't say a word. Ryan was taken aback by Rich's body language and worried he had pushed his friend too far.

At last, Rich couldn't continue the charade any longer and let out a burst of laughter.

"Had you going, didn't I?" Rich teased.

Ryan dropped the list and propped his feet on the desk. "Why do I always fall for that routine?" Ryan waded up the list and threw it in

Rich's direction.

Rich swatted the paper out of the air before it hit him between the eyes. He smiled. "You've always been gullible. That's one of your enduring traits."

"So, I get the feeling you've already met Alana."

"Correct! I met the charming innkeeper this morning when I booked a room for three weeks. With my busy schedule, I thought it would be simpler to stay in town."

"Three weeks!" Ryan rubbed his hands together in anticipation of a possible match. "That's fantastic! You'll definitely get to know one another in that length of time."

"Stop it! You look like you're making an evil plan instead of trying your hand as a marriage broker."

Rich wasn't about to confess his first impressions of Alana. He also wouldn't admit that he was confused about the overwhelming, irresistible attraction he'd felt in her presence. He needed to process his thoughts before he shared them with anyone—even his best friend.

Ryan knew it was time to drop the subject. The next few minutes they spent time catching up on news they'd missed during social distancing.

***

Rich drove home in his candy apple red 1940 Ford pickup. It was his prized possession—a treasure from the past. He called her Betsy, christened his grandfather. She had been in the family for so long, Betsy was considered part of the family. Rich had no idea when he restored the vintage truck, sixteen years prior, it would be the perfect vehicle for his new holiday gig, spreading Christmas cheer to boys and girls. The old truck was part of his family story.

Rich stopped for a quick gas 'n' go before leaving Spring Valley. He decided to avoid the quick interstate route to Bristol. He wasn't in a hurry. Plus, he didn't want a speed laser gun pointed at his vehicle. He had a heavy foot. He knew he wasn't the only speedster; everyone breaks the speed limit law, by a little or a lot. Usually, it's harmless speeding, just trying to keep up with the traffic flow. Most ordinary drivers don't have the skill or courage to drive fast. Rich had both—a reality he always considered.

He took the backroad through Piney Flats because he wanted to think. As he drove in his shiny red truck, his mind took him on a heritage drive.

Since his earliest memories, fast cars were part of his life—part of his DNA. Stock car racing had its roots in Appalachia. Two years before Prohibition ended, as soon as his granddaddy's feet reached the pedals, he was inducted into the family bootlegging business, transporting moonshine out of the holler on winding backroads in his family's Ford coupe. After Rich's granddaddy returned home from

WWII, he purchased the 1940 Ford pickup for the family farm and his side business—running hooch. The repeal of Prohibition didn't hinder Appalachian moonshining—it prospered and provided salvation for his cash-strapped folks, back in the hills. The high federal alcohol taxes and dry counties, where the local government forbid the sales of any kind of alcoholic beverages, kept the bootleggers running the backroads. A self-taught mechanic, his granddaddy added the Cadillac V8 engine, discreetly lowered the truck body, just enough so it wouldn't draw any unwanted attention, and kept on truckin' his bootleg-market business. He could outrun any Revenuer in hot pursuit. During those daring chases, his granddaddy discovered his talent behind the wheel, which led him to the lure of stock car racing to make few extra bucks. His granddaddy overhauled the old Ford Coupe, the original moonshine running vehicle, and tried his hand at racing. Rich's father continued the tradition, tearing up dirt tracks across the South. He was no Jimmy Johnson, but Rich's father spent time trading paint with the best of them. Rich knew at an early age that racing was in his blood. His granddaddy eventually handed down the old truck to his only grandson.

Rich and Ryan cruised the streets of Bristol during their high school days in his coveted ride. Betsy had speed, she could beat anyone who dared to challenge him, yet she wouldn't win any awards at a Truck Show. After Rich married and left his hometown for North Carolina to pursue his racing career, the truck sat abandoned in the barn for twenty years.

Restoring the truck was added to Rich's bucket list. When Rich had the luxury of cash and a case of sentimentality, he began the process. Restoring metal and memories. Precious memories. Memories of his dad and himself tinkering on the engine—a reminder of who really prepared him for his path to success. His first DUI —a reminder of his human failures. Memories of being snuggled up in the front seat at a drive-in movie with his young bride—a reminder of the power of love.

His restored treasure ended up being in between a show piece and a daily driver. His classic car garage and workshop served as a safe haven for Rich's high-tech backup truck, a 2022 Ford F-150 Raptor, along with his rare 1963 Sting Ray split-window Corvette, and a wide collection of classic sports cars. After he cut out alcohol, collecting cars became his vice—a weakness that didn't destroy him. He loved fast cars, but for him, it was always about Betsy, that 1940 Ford pickup, loaded down with memories. Rich smiled, thinking of the paradox that his hands held the steering wheel his granddaddy once gripped while running moonshine, and now, it transported Rich to his recovery meeting.

As he drove with his memories of long

ago, Alana entered his thoughts. He wondered if a second chance of love was in his future. He daydreamed picking her up at the inn on a fall afternoon. She steps up in the truck cab and scoots close beside him. The wind blowing through an open window, tousling her hair, she brushes it back, turns and smiles...

He shook his head to bring himself back to reality. *Get control of yourself.* He was perplexed how such a brief encounter with Alana made such a lasting impression. Usually, when it came to the thoughts of romance, he was always cautious and careful, today, not so much. His best friend was right when he said that Rich didn't have to live life alone. Rich also knew that loneliness was a choice he'd made. He decided he might take a risk with the innkeeper and throw caution to the wind. His foot pushed heavier on the gas pedal. He drove on with optimism.

Chapter Five

The break of day was Ada's favorite time at the Mockingbird Coffee House. It offered the refreshing promise of new beginnings. Ada couldn't remember when she didn't start her days at the crack of dawn. Today was like any other day. Early to bed, early to rise. For many of Ada's former colleagues, retirement included fulfilling the dream to travel the world in their golden years. The wanderlust bug never bit Ada or her husband, J.R. They were hometown-lovers. Content to spend their days in Appalachia, where they had deep rooted connections to their ancestor's culture, faith, and family that went as far back as the late 1700s when the pioneers settled in the foothills of the Appalachian Mountains and brought their slaves with them. Ada enjoyed her second-act as a business owner.

She made a quick trip inside to retrieve a broom. She returned outside and stopped in her steps on the porch to study the grandeur of the historic church building, overlooking downtown Spring Valley—like a magnificent guardian angel spreading its wings of protection over the little town. She whispered a prayer of thanksgiving for the privilege and blessing to be the caretaker of this hallowed ground. It was overwhelming at times. She reflected over the past year when she feared history was repeating itself. During the cholera pandemic of 1873, the congregation literally died out and closed its doors. The coffee house wasn't a casualty of the recent pandemic, but she spent many sleepless nights on her knees in prayer.

Broom in hand, Ada stood on the threshold, faced outward and began sweeping the entryway clean of dust, leaves, and sparkling cobwebs on which the spiders spent overtime spinning their creation the night before. Ada remembered the African American blessing her great-grandmother taught her: *Sweep to keep wickedness or sickness away from the front door to protect the family*. Ada always prayed for protection of her community family. She and J.R. were childless, but as a teacher, she felt blessed in having a small part in helping raise kids in her classroom. After retirement, her family expanded to her coffee house community where she dedicated her life to paying it forward, always listening, and obeying God's whispers. She became a devout emissary of hope.

Admiring the building wasn't going to get the fresh-from-the-oven bake goods baked. Ada scolded herself. Since the coffee house didn't have a modern drive-thru that opened at sunup, Ada's loyal customers started moseying in between 8 a.m. and 9 a.m. Fortunately, business was picking up with Ada appreciating busy times, again. She headed inside to enjoy the silence of her sanctuary before being joined by the early-morning staff.

Ada planned a break in her afternoon in order to meet with Shauna and Gabe to finalize the wedding-day timeline for their ceremony at the coffee house. The big event fell on December 25th—the perfect day for Shauna's Christmas crazy family. Thanks to Shauna's mother's business, The Olde Town Christmas Shop, Shauna lived a 24/7 Christmas life. It was enchanting as a child, but Ada watched as Shauna grew tired of the fantasy world when she moved into her teenage years. It tickled Ada to think that Shauna's romance revolved around her dreaded holiday and to see Shauna's mother in holiday heaven, planning her youngest daughter's Christmas themed wedding. It was perfect timing for Ada as well. She had planned a long, four-day, holiday weekend off for her staff. Shauna's and Gabe's families would take care of set-up and tear-down so Wednesday morning, it would be ready for business, like nothing out of the ordinary had ever happened. Nothing was ordinary about the couple's journey. Ada thought it might just be one of the most romantic adventures she had ever witnessed, except maybe her own. She knew she was a little biased; after all, she claimed divine intervention when she felt the Lord used her as his emissary matchmaker when she *"randomly"* drew their names and teamed them together to sponsor a wishing ornament from the Giving Tree. Gabe and Shauna's happily-ever-after started that very night, almost two years to the date.

Ada was so proud of the Giving Tree, a tradition she began several years ago when she placed a tree in the coffee house and decorated it with an eclectic variety of ornaments tied to the branches with colorful ribbons. Anyone in the community was invited to fill out a Christmas wish request and tie the little scroll on an ornament. The concept was different than most gifting trees. The request couldn't be for yourself, and volunteers who took the request were not allowed to accomplish the task on their own. They were only facilitators. They had to recruit other volunteers to help make the hopeful wishes come true.

Like every community in the country, the shutdown took an immense toll in the Appalachian region. Ada anticipated the branches on the tree would bend, loaded with hope-filled wishing ornaments this year.

For the pasts few weeks, she tossed another idea around in her head and landed on the concept of expanding the Giving Tree project to include a Memory Tree—a decorated tree adorned to reflect the life of loved ones lost. Her heart broke when the coffee house reopened, and many of her regulars were gone forever—counted among the lost. The local ladies who gathered for their afternoon tea lost two of their own, and her kind, generous, insurance agent succumbed to the virus.

There were headstones added to the cemetery, yet most had no funerals to morn their loss. The Memory Tree would be a joint community memorial, and she'd ask J.R. to hold a brief celebration of life service at the coffee house. She knew the event would be somber to see a tree adorned with pictures and memorabilia honoring precious lives lost, but at least, she thought, they would not be forgotten.

In recent years, the Giving Tree had renewed a present-day movement of generosity in Spring Valley. The act of giving was a tie that bound the town folks together. A scripture came to Ada's mind: *See that you also excel in this grace of giving.* Ada knew, firsthand, that Spring Valley always excelled in giving. The community had a long history in giving and rebuilding with ordinary, everyday folk trying to help and bless their neighbors.

Ada was proud of her community's generosity history. A spring located a few blocks from the coffee house led to the establishment of Spring Valley, providing a life-giving water source for generations. Early pioneers carved out a settlement, coming together to build log homes with fell trees from the adjacent forests. Eventually, townsfolks saw brick, stone, or well-framed houses and businesses lining the long main street.

Ada especially appreciated the history of the tiny print shop that was devoted solely to the abolishment of human slavery, where a large number of free blacks in Spring Valley were co-existing in the early 1800s. The foothills of the Appalachian Mountains became a stronghold for the abolitionist cause of giving freedom to all enslaved people.

A choleric pandemic of 1873 nearly wiped out the town. More than once, fires consumed downtown buildings, but did not extinguish the spirit of survival as the townspeople came together to rebuild. Ada was a witness. That spirit still exists today. She was confident whatever wishes hung on the Giving Tree would be fulfilled this Christmas, and the Memory Tree would be a celebration of life, in loving memory of the unique lives of the dearly departed and the legacy they left behind.

***

The afternoon lull at the coffee house gave Ada the opportune time to meet with Shauna and Gabe. Ada arranged to meet them at the newly formed women's rescue ministry. For years, Ada dreamed of their church opening a safe house to provide rescue, shelter, and hope for at risk women and their children. She knew, firsthand, there was a need. On many occasions, she and J.R. had offered their home to shelter defenseless women and children who were victims of domestic violence. The church didn't have the finances to fund another ministry. The church board fought Ada and wanted her to give up on her dream, which she wouldn't abandon. She also never gave up on asking God for His blessing. She knew it was all in His timing. The time arrived when a faithful church member left startup funds and a large historic home in a trust to be used as a women's shelter. It was perfect! At one time, the house had been renovated as a bed and breakfast. It had five large bedrooms, each with their own private ensuite bathroom. It was fully furnished, a turn-key opportunity to launch the Haven House ministry.

The shelter was within walking distance of the coffee house. Ada was the queen of recruiting volunteers. She believed whole heartedly in seeing and believing. It's one thing to read about domestic violence in the headlines, but it's another to face *reality* with your own eyes. This would give Ada the opportunity to share the ministry's vision.

Ada left the coffee house a little early to give her time to chat a few minutes with the house director and to let her know she was bringing guests. Ada knew the director always welcomed volunteers to assist with the workload. Ada also wanted to say hello to the residents and make a few phone calls to try locating an essential item desperately needed for one of the new mothers. A baby formula shortage was hitting families hard. Between supply chain issues, severe weather delivery disruptions, and a recent recall of a similar prescription-only formula, the demand for baby formula for babies with allergies had skyrocketed. Ada's mission was to secure baby formula.

The Haven House blended in with all the other historic homes in Spring Valley. There was no signage, not anything that would indicate it was a shelter. Ada had a key and the code to the security system, but for extra safety measures, she always rang the doorbell twice, followed by four loud knocks on the front door. She could hear people talking in the house and children laughing and playing in the back yard. Today, they were happy sounds. As she stood waiting on the porch, she whispered a prayer of blessing.

At the volunteers' desk, after making unsuccessful phone calls, Ada went over the '4-5 Weeks to Go' wedding planning checklist she'd downloaded from a website. She was sure Shauna had everything under control, but Ada had a few questions that needed answered. Ada had attended dozens of weddings, but since this was her first time to officiate, she was a little nervous.

Belinda Graham, the house director, welcomed Gabe and Shauna and walked them to the original parlor, now used as a makeshift office for volunteers and a designated homeschooling room. Ada greeted them from the desk that was tucked in the corner beside the fireplace. She gestured for them to have a seat.

"This place is amazing!" Shauna stood in

the middle of the room surveying every nook and cranny. Her eyes lingered on the Bible verse decoration on the wall: *God's safe-house for the battered, a sanctuary during bad times.* It tugged at her heart.

Colorful individual bins filled with crayons, pencils, glue sticks, calculators, rulers, art material —whatever supplies and curriculum needed for homeschooling, filled the beautiful built-in bookshelves. A dry erase board with math problems awaited pupils. Traditional student desks and chairs were lined up in a row, just as Shauna remembered from elementary school.

"I hope you didn't mind meeting me here. I've been wanting to introduce you to the ministry." Ada's face lit up.

Gabe pulled off his jacket and scooted the chairs around to Ada's workstation. "No, this was no problem at all. We are so excited your vision for this ministry came to pass." He looked around wondering if they would be in the way. "Are you sure we won't be disturbing the flow of things this afternoon?"

Ada assured him, "No, we're fine. Homeschooling is over for the day. The kids are outside playing. We have volunteers and moms in the kitchen getting dinner ready."

"I never imagined a homeschool in a shelter. I just assumed the children went to regular classes in the local school." Shauna pulled out a chair and sat behind a student desk. "Does this bring back memories, Miss Ada? Me fidgeting and you standing at the chalk board, giving me the stink eye."

Ada laughed. "Yes, you were such a precocious child. I knew the combination of being exceptionally smart and little sassy would take you far in life."

Gabe joined in. "I'm sure you've heard the saying *redheads are sunshine mixed with hurricane,*" Gabe teased. "That was written with Shauna in mind."

Ada responded to Shauna's insight about the homeschool. "From our experience, for a woman fleeing a violent situation, homeschooling is the safest option for the children." Just in case there were any children within the sound of her voice, Ada almost whispered. "From my network of educators, we have certified teachers in a type of homeschooling co-op that volunteer to teach. The teachers have been an incredible blessing, not only to the children, but also to their mothers."

"How many can you shelter?" Gabe asked.

"We have five-bedroom suites, but one is designated to the overnight caretaker. We can house four women. Usually, they have two or three children. Needless to say, it can be a full house."

"I know you had a trust set up to start the ministry, but I'm sure you're constantly in need of finances." Shauna took a seat beside Gabe and reached over to hold his hand.

Ada loved to see compassion swell up in a

heart. "Yes, those funds are designated to full time staff and expenses to maintain the home. But, there's always special needs. Our house director and the overnight caretakers are paid staff, and the rest of the duties falls on the shoulders of volunteers." Ada shared her philosophy on fund raising. "I'm a strong believer in asking God to provide our needs. But I also seek volunteers to testify how God uses the safe house, not only to offer a safe harbor from physical harm, but to show them how God's love and protection will guide them throughout their life. Nothing is more powerful than friends asking friends to give."

"Count me in." Shauna raised her hand. "You know my skills in social media marketing and web design. Once we get settled in after the wedding, you can count on me."

Gabe wasn't sure how he might enlist his help; he assumed most volunteers were women.

As he pondered, a little boy made a mad dash into the room with his mom in close pursuit. Gabe guessed the boy would be around five years old.

"I'm so sorry; he escaped." A frazzled young woman scooped him up in her arms. The boy laughed and tried to wriggle his way down.

Ada assured her it was no problem.

The little guy immediately captured Gabe's heart. When he exited the room with his mom, Gabe surrendered. "Sign me up."

Shauna pulled out her laptop from her backpack. "Let's get down to wedding business."

"It's crunch time, let's go!" Gabe chimed in, even though he knew he was only along for the ride.

The next half hour they decided on their wedding vows, the ceremony, confirmed arrival times, and finalized the wedding timeline. Shauna shut her laptop. "We've got this."

Ada decided to see what Shauna and Gabe thought about her idea of the Memory Tree and proceeded to share the details.

Gabe was the first to respond, "I would love to place an ornament on the tree for my former neighbor, Mr. Barkley." Gabe remembered the Christmas he helped Mrs. Barkley hang wreaths on her home. Before the pandemic, Mr. Barkley had been diagnosed with Alzheimer's. Gabe knew it broke Mrs. Barkley's heart when her beloved had to be moved to a nursing home. She was devastated when he passed away. "After her husband's passing, Mrs. Barkley moved out-of-state to live with her daughter. I know that she would be honored that her husband will be remembered."

"I think it's such a sweet idea. Once you have all the details, send me an email, and I'll post it on Facebook and start getting the word out," Shauna volunteered.

Ada was humbled that they would squeeze in one more activity in their already hectic schedule. She followed them out to their Jeep and hugged them good-bye. "I guess the next time I'll see you two will be at the rehearsal dinner."

As Ada walked back to the Mockingbird Coffee House, she knew the beautiful old church building would be a perfect venue. She hoped and prayed for a true picturesque winter wedding with a powdery-white backdrop brimming with snow, romance, and love. She couldn't ask for more.

Chapter Six

The room was dark. Ada's internal clock woke her before the buzzing sound had a chance. She glanced at the alarm on her nightstand, and she was glad she had a few minutes before her feet would touch the floor. Ada lay motionless listening to J.R. sleep. His arm rested on her waist. Ada always felt safe in his arms.

In sleep, J.R. wrestled with his emotions. Exhausted, frustrated, and lonely; his mind struggled to make sense of the upended world they'd lived in for so long. Even as he slept, his forehead furrowed. Ada wished she could erase the worry. All she could do was love him and pray. She did both, fervently. She whispered a scripture, *"Don't worry about anything; instead pray about everything."*

Careful not to wake him, Ada slipped from the bed and wrapped her housecoat around her before she left the room.

Groggy from another restless night, J.R. woke discombobulated. The scent of bacon brought him to reality. Ada was in the kitchen. It must be Sunday, he thought, because she only fried bacon on Sundays. She was humming a hymn. He could visualize her in her hair bonnet, wrapped in a well-worn housecoat moving seamlessly around the room. He heard running water, then her pouring it in the coffee maker. Dishes clanked as she gathered them to set the table. J.R. scrunched his face in anticipation of the sound of shattering glass, but he was wrong. He knew she attempted to be quiet, but no one would ever describe Ada as dainty or delicate. She was more of a bull-in-a-china-shop kind of gal. But, oh, how he loved her!

J.R. was so tired. Pastoring had been a challenge in the last couple of years. He struggled to see beyond the heartache and pain so many experienced. He was thankful that he had Ada to lean on. She was his rock. She made him whole. He thought of how it had always been—Ada and me, forever. He felt comfort in knowing that they were both right with their Creator, and they were right with each other. They had been best friends, sharing memories for over forty years.

He looked over at the scripture plaque that sat on his nightstand. *What is your life? For you are a mist that appears for a little time, then vanishes.*

J.R. asks and answers that question to start each day. Sometimes aloud, sometimes to himself. He closed his eyes and answered in his heart and mind, *I'm here to tell and live Christ's story. I want to spend my days blessing others.*

He had witnessed sadness in ministry but never like this. The pandemic did not discriminate, it was no respecter of persons. During the height of the outbreak, that verse was so poignant—so many had stepped into eternity, leaving their mist of life.

J.R. knew he wasn't alone in his struggle. This was not the way pastors were intended to do ministry. Wounded and stressed, he reached out to an online platform and met with other leaders that helped him in his time of crisis. It was a life saver. J.R. became more confident in his calling, identified new areas for ministry, and held on to hope. A scripture came to his mind: *For you have been my hope, Lord, my confidence since my youth.* He sat on the edge of the bed, stretched his stiff shoulders, searched out his slippers with his right foot, and strolled into the kitchen in his pajamas.

***

"Good morning, sunshine!" Ada greeted him with a quick peck on the cheek. "Perfect timing, I was just getting ready to take the biscuits out of the oven."

J.R. grabbed his mug from the table and headed for the coffee maker. He leaned on the counter as he stirred his sweetener and cream, smiled, and said, "Okay, but first coffee." He took a sip and savored the dark roast brew in his favorite blessed coffee mug with the inspirational quote, *Good Days Start with Coffee & Jesus.*

Sunday breakfast was a treat. Ada closed the coffee house on Sundays which allowed time for cooking up a hearty Southern breakfast, complete with homemade biscuits and gravy, bacon, grits, and scrambled cheese-eggs. It made the kitchen feel all warm and cozy. It was the best way to start their busy day.

Ada was a spur-of-the-moment sort of person. J.R. never knew what the topic of conversation would be around the table. In the middle of their morning meal, when she sat her fork down, leaned back in the chair, and took a breath, he knew something was coming and more than likely, that *something* involved him.

"Yesterday, I met with Gabe and Shauna to go over last-minute details for the wedding."

"How did that go? It will be here before you know it." J.R. spread strawberry jam on his final biscuit.

"It went great. I shared an idea with them and wanted to know what you thought."

There it was. He thought.

"What's that, hon?" He studied her face.

Ada proceeded to lay out her idea for the Memory Tree. From her description, J.R. knew it wasn't an idea she just had 'in mind.' It was a meticulous, thought-out plan she was in the process of executing, and the success would definitely include his participation. He nodded in agreement, even cocked his eyebrow a couple of times, anticipating the ask. Then it came.

"Our congregation wasn't spared from loss. I know how tremendously hard this crisis has been on you. During sickness and death, you have been a strong shoulder to lean on." She continued and reached over and touched his hand, "You couldn't bring a eulogy during the pandemic, but you could hold a brief community memorial service at the coffee house now to honor the ones we've lost."

Giving her husband time to respond, Ada picked up her fork for another bite of biscuits and gravy. She chased it with a gulp of orange juice, anticipating some type of acknowledgement from J.R. It took longer than she expected. She hoped it wasn't too depressing of a subject to discuss this early.

'Well, I have to admit, I didn't anticipate this topic for breakfast." J.R. slowly wiped his mouth with his napkin. "I may have to think on this for a while."

"What's there to think about?" Ada was always impetuous.

It was a great idea, but J.R. was concerned Ada was adding too much to her already full schedule. "Let's just think about what you've got going on." He held up his hand and started counting with his thumb and finished with his pinky. "Firstly, the coffee house is almost back to full swing, you're understaffed and filling those hours yourself; secondly, you are hosting and officiating Gabe and Shauna's wedding; thirdly, you have the Giving Tree project, and let's not forget the women's shelter; and last, but not least; church activities." They sat side-by-side at the table, close enough for him to lean in and hold up all five fingers to her face. His interrogation continued. "How do you plan to pull this off in this short amount of time?"

He immediately saw the sparkle in her eyes and anticipated her response. He knew she had him just where she wanted.

Ada smiled and said, "With your help, of course." She proceeded to tell him how he could announce the Memory Tree project at church this morning and start recruiting volunteers. She already had flyers printed with all the details to distribute.

She stood and framed his face with her hands. She leaned in and kissed him on the lips. A kiss that made his pulse race. *It wasn't fair*. He thought.

Ada was certain he couldn't say no.

J.R. knew his holiday schedule just got a lot more complicated.

Chapter Seven

It was almost dusk when Rich took a break from packing and stepped out on to the front porch. Outside, Rich bent over and set the automatic timer connected to his porch decorations and Christmas yard ornaments. He was sorry he had disappointed Debbie the decorator. Every year she had full access to the property—inside and out, to create the perfect holiday scene. Since Rich would be in Spring Valley most of the month, he decided this year outside trimmings would suffice. From her email reply, Debbie was doubly disappointed that he was not going to be home to assist. On several occasions, Debbie let him know she was interested in being more than a decorator. He'd politely refused a dozen 'let's do coffee' invitations. He didn't think she was The One, so he didn't want to waste his or her time. As he flipped on the switch, his porch came alive. He had to admit she was a great holiday designer as he admired the menagerie of Christmas décor welcoming the season.

When Rich patted the lifelike black Labrador puppy statue, bundled up with a festive scarf around its neck, the motion sensor brought the pup to life and played Christmas songs as its head moved and lights blinked to the music. The five-foot-tall musical nutcracker stood watch at the grand entrance door, adorned with triple wreaths connected by velvety red ribbons and garland draped over the sash. Bright red illuminated Santa boots, with faux fur tops and leather straps with a buckle, that sat on the doormat. One would surmise Santa lived here and left his boots out to dry. Rich smiled, thinking their assumption would be correct.

He shoved his hands in his jacket pockets and walked out to inspect the yard. He scanned the over-sized yard ornaments—just as he anticipated, one was missing. He shook his head. "I can't believe I hired a decorator who refuses a client's request," he murmured. Every year, she somehow conveniently forgets to include his vintage plastic Santa because—it *didn't blend in with the décor*.

Since Debbie never bothered to ask the story behind the shabby plastic Santa, Rich didn't bother to share.

Rich retrieved from storage the old plastic Santa with a bag full of toys slung over his shoulder and placed it amongst the fancy decorations. He wasn't embarrassed by the shabby Santa that sat in front of his mini mansion. It was a reminder. A reminder of how far he'd come. He stood a moment, his mind occupied with memories. Growing up in Appalachia, Rich's dad didn't have much to offer his kids, but the plastic

Santa with a painted twinkle in his eye always gave the family joy. It had a way of illuminating the spirit of Christmas. It was one of the good memories of his dad. After his parents passed away, Rich found the old familiar plastic Santa stashed away in a shed. His dad's most treasured possession had seen better days. The paint chipped and the color faded, but it still sparked the joy of Christmas in Rich's heart—the reason he transformed into jolly old Saint Nick year after year.

The valley was oddly quiet in November. The Ramsey farm, located a mile down the road from the Bristol Motor Speedway, was where his ancestors made their home. When the speedway was built in 1961, neighbors' farms were snatched up for the humongous project, but the family farm missed out on the action—it was just a little too far away. Rich grew up in the shadow of the racetrack with championship dreams that led him to the industry. The thunderous sounds of racing echoed around the mountains and settled in the valley, giving it the Thunder Valley nickname. The blasting noise caused many to eventually sell their homes, but it was fuel that ignited Rich's career. Today, the valley held silence.

Success changed the exterior of the farm. It was no longer a working farm. When Rich's dad decided there would be more money in a campground than a fledgling homestead, Rich financed the transition from a working farm to a family campground for race fans, complete with full R.V. hookups, tent camping, and shuttle service to the race. When he retired from racing, he preferred watching races on the big screen at the campground with die-hard fans. After retirement, Rich built his mini mansion on the far end of the property, tucked up at the foothill of a mountain. It was a status symbol. Everyone that made it in the industry built a mansion. Status didn't seem that important to him, never was—so he regretted building such a large home because he rattled around alone in that big house. Truth be told, he preferred his cozy houseboat on Lady Lake. Rich remodeled his parents' home for a guest house. He never imagined himself returning to the family farm. Success made changes—the cars he drove, the house he lived in, the money he spent —but much remained the same. It was the family farm. The land passed down from generation to generation. It was home.

The vibration of Rich's phone interrupted his thoughts. It was a text.

Ainsley: *Hi! Look forward to 2NT!*

Rich: *See you there.*

He preferred phone conversations over text messaging, Rich thought with a furrowed brow as he put his phone back in his pocket. Text abbreviations were always a guessing game for him. He also didn't know how to interpret emojis. As a sponsor in Celebrate Recovery, he had mentored dozens of individuals over the years, but this was his first attempt at being a 'virtual' sponsor. Thanks to technology, during the shutdown, virtual coaching became more common and a much-needed lifeline. Tonight, he would meet Ainsley in person. Tonight, he would introduce himself to his group. The same greeting —confession, he uttered dozens of times.

Hello everyone! My name is Rich. I'm a grateful believer in Jesus who struggles with alcohol.

The task following him now was that he had to finish packing for his extended stay at Spring Valley Inn. Normally, he would just throw in jeans and his Santa suit, but he had the wedding rehearsal dinner, he needed his workout clothes, and he had to consider Alana. She had been on his mind for nineteen days—even his dreams. Tomorrow, he grinned at his own thoughts. Tomorrow, he would be in the company of Alana. Tomorrow, no dreams, a real face-to-face conversation. One, he anticipated, one of many.

Chapter Eight

I t took her nearly an hour to get dressed for the evening. Alana twirled around and looked over her shoulder at her reflection. She loved the dress. It had a gypsy flare. Very soft and feminine. She found it at her favorite boutique in Asheville. Alana never left that shop empty handed. "Turquoise dangle earrings or teardrop leaf wooden hoops?" She held one up to each ear.

"The turquoise will accent the flecks in your green eyes." Jean was stunned her sister asked her fashion advice.

Always the Chef, Jean protested wearing anything but her uniform. Even though she was the mother of the groom, she had to prepare and serve the dinner guests. Her sous chef, Craig, would be on hand, but she was still in charge and honored to host her son's rehearsal dinner. Jean compromised and gave in to Alana's request that Jean at least change into a freshly laundered jacket, prior to guests' arrival.

Before she left the room, Jean prodded her sister. "You seem a little nervous."

"Nervous. Why would I be nervous?"

"I don't know, you tell me. You haven't

shown interest in a man for ages. Whenever you chat with Ada, I've noticed you've been casually inquiring about Rich. Thought maybe you had him on your mind since it's taken you forever to choose a dress."

"I admit, I'm a little anxious. When he checked in this afternoon, I felt like a high school girl with a crush on the new guy. It was awkward. There's just something special about him."

She put her arm around Alana's shoulder and squeezed. "I don't think you have anything to be nervous about, just enjoy the evening. Maybe this is the first night of a holiday romance." Jean winked as she headed down to the kitchen. Then she transformed into big, bossy sister mode. "Hurry up, you're going to be late."

Alana blamed the tardiness on having to share a bathroom with her sister. Originally, when they purchased the inn, the plan was for Chef Jean to move into the large innkeeper suite, and Alana would find an apartment within walking distance to the inn. When the inn was shut down during the pandemic, Alana needed to pinch pennies and occupied an empty guest room that wasn't generating income. Eventually, when the restrictions were lifted, in order to save money, Alana and Jean decided to divide the innkeeper suite into two bedrooms. The only drawback was sharing a bathroom—just as they did in their youth. Which never made sense to Alana. Their childhood home was a mansion in Boston's most famous historic neighborhood of Beacon Hill, with five bathrooms. However, their mother decided their bathroom would be sandwiched between their two bedrooms, accessible by both rooms. Their mother claimed she shared a *powder room* with her sister, which she felt brought them closer together. Alana's aunt died before Alana was born, so she didn't know much about her aunt, but guessed that her mother and aunt must have had the same personality traits in order to share such a confined, private space—which beyond any doubt, was not the case with Alana and Jean. They were complete opposites. Alana's side of the vanity was organized, clean, and uncluttered. Jean's side was messy, dirty, and untidy. Which was such a contradiction in itself because once Jean entered the kitchen and put on her chef's hat, she transformed into her over-the-top organized alter ego. Alana, grinned thinking how Jean refers to it as *mise en place*, the French culinary phrase for *putting in place* or *gather*, which Jean claims is the foundation for a successfully run kitchen. Alana looked in the mirror and mimicked her sister in a French accent, "*Mise en place.*" She hoped Jean wasn't within earshot. As Alana cleared off the vanity, wiped it down, and stored everything under the sink, she wished Jean would wear her chef's hat in the bathroom.

***

Alana slipped into her heels and hurried downstairs. The table was set in the formal dining room with Shauna's grandmother's desirable Appalachian folk art Christmas dishes. It was Thanksgiving evening, but the wedding and rehearsal had a Christmas theme.

Alana loved the charming, vintage, hand-painted collectors' pottery. Women were recruited from 'up in the hills' to create the works of art. Shauna's grandmother was one of those women. In the late 1940s, her grandmother could not afford to purchase any of the dishes she created, but she eventually splurged and bought the colorful red poinsettia pattern dishes that became a family heirloom. The mantle was decorated with fresh greenery, gold candles, and the bride's favorite whimsical carved ornaments. The fire was lit, warming the room before the honored guest arrived.

Alana surveyed the room, reviewed centerpieces, place settings, level of the music, and made sure everything was perfect for Gabe and Shauna's rehearsal dinner. Gabe officially claimed the title of nephew, but unofficially, Alana was a second mother to him, and she treated him as if he were her own son.

While making sure the *Private Party* sign was secured on the dining room door, Alana was the first to greet Gabe and Shauna, as they entered the lobby.

"We're a little early," Shauna began when Alana reached for her coat. "I wanted to be the first to see the decorations." Shauna led Gabe by the hand to the dining room.

"Amazing! It's beautiful." Shauna gestured toward the mantle. "You even have the little carved red bird ornaments." Missing her Gran, Shauna blinked away the tears and recited the mountain saying, "When cardinals appear, angels are near."

"Your mom dropped off your grandmother's dishes and the ornaments. She said they were a must. I think they look lovely," Alana assured her.

Gabe wrapped his long arms around his aunt in a warm embrace. "Thank you for co-hosting the rehearsal. I hope you know how much we love you."

"Stop right there," Alana warned, "we'll all be weeping willows." Alana heard the jingle from the bell on the front entrance door and excused herself. "I'll greet who's entered."

Once the dinner guests arrived, the tranquil dining room atmosphere bustled with laughter, hugs, and excitement. One voice carried above others—Ada's. Alana loved Ada's charming, relaxed tempo. It was comforting and trustworthy. Tonight was a momentous night in Ada's matchmaking hobby. And Ada knew how to enjoy every minute of every day.

Alana kept glancing toward the stairway. Rich was late—beyond fashionably late. He was the only one missing from the guest list. She wouldn't delay the festivities. She stepped in the kitchen to find Jean removing her apron, signaling it was time to dine. Unbeknownst to Alana, Rich had joined the party.

Chef Jean introduced her assistants, Craig and Cydney, took off her chef's hat, took on her role as mother of the groom, and joined the wedding party. Gabe kissed his mom on both cheeks. Jean took a deep breath and relaxed. The menu needed no explanation because the aroma drifting from the kitchen wafted the smell of the sea.

"I am so honored to co-host and prepare the rehearsal dinner this evening," Jean cleared her throat, choking back the tears. "Tonight's menu is filled with special requests from the bride and groom. A sentimental food experience, if you will." Jean glanced toward Gabe. "Would you like to explain?"

"As you can imagine, with me, a Northerner, and Shauna raised in the South, our food palate is vastly different. Our first meal at the inn was the result of a challenge that she would try my clam chowder if I tried her cheesy grits and pimento cheese." Gabe shook his head in disgust.

"You're not telling the whole story," Shauna interrupted. "I was bamboozled. When you invited me to dinner, you didn't mention the full menu." Shauna lovingly teased her fiancé.

"If I had, I feared you wouldn't come."

"Oh, I would have come." She held her hand to her heart.

"Aw, that's so romantic." Abby chimed in. She found her sister's love story dreamy.

"That night, as I sat across the table from

this gorgeous woman, I realized that I had found love. Two years ago, when Shauna arrived home for the holidays, hope came to town. My hope. Tonight's meal is a re-creation of the items served that magical evening." Gabe bent down to kiss Shauna as applause broke out.

Chef Jean was a genius at reinterpreting classic foods. It didn't concern Gabe that the food would be prepared differently; he knew his mother's creations would be one hundred times better.

Cydney entered the dining room with a full appetizer plate of pimento cheese phyllo cups. Shauna was the first to bite into the buttery, flaky pastry shells filled with creamy and warm pimento cheese dip, sprinkled with bits of bacon. "These are incredible! I didn't know pimento cheese could be so fancy!" Shauna raved.

Her future mother-in-law humbly accepted the accolade.

As Cydney and Craig dished the clam chowder, Alana assisted in serving drinks. "Would you like some wine?" She smiled at Rich.

Rich surprised her in his choice. "No, I would prefer tea."

She sat the wine bottle down on the table and walked toward the doorway of the kitchen. She turned and asked, "Sweet tea or artificial sweetener?" She assumed sweetener since his body fat was nil.

"Artificial, please."

She was gone, but the scent of her perfume lingered. An intoxicating feminine floral bouquet. He couldn't pinpoint the exact flower, but the fragrance whispered romance.

Her absence felt like eternity. He kept glancing at the kitchen door. Was her delay intentional? A punishment for his tardiness? Rich studied. He wanted to but couldn't explain the reason for his delay. The role of a sponsor required being available in times of crisis or relapse. He had to take the phone call. Anonymity and confidentiality were required.

She dawdled. Alana saw him glance at the door when Cydney retrieved a dish from the kitchen. My goodness, he's attractive, she thought as she poured the tea. An incredible sweater choice, she critiqued. It was Italian. An elegant, black cashmere-silk, quarter zip polo sweater with a gold contrast trim on the collar. The cut of the sweater and his black designer jeans were perfect for his athletic physique. For theatrics, she decided to take her *own sweet time*. She liked that Southern saying and used often. He could wait a few more minutes. Tit for tat. Plus, she needed her pulse to slow.

Rich checked his watch and wondered where the tea was, Bristol? He softly drummed his fingers on the table. He waited. How was he going to approach this potential relationship? Rich would much prefer an uncomplicated romance. Nothing in his life had ever been easy, he supposed.

Why would this be any different? She was complex. Alana may be out of his league. He ceased the battle in his head. Stop making assumptions, Rich told himself.

Her black party leather heels clacking on the antique hardwood, Alana sashayed out of the kitchen. She stole his breath. She was a woman in charge. A mix of sophistication and sass. Her stride, slow and deliberate, made her long floating dress lend a playful movement. His pulse raced. Rich resolved. He liked a challenge.

"I'm sorry for the delay." She smiled. She knew she didn't need forgiveness. She was just being polite. She placed his tea on the table, pulled out the empty dinning chair, and seated herself beside him. He took that as a positive sign.

They dined on buttered lobster, spicy chorizo, fingerling potatoes, little neck clams, and sweet corn puree. "Your sister is a magnificent chef," Rich casually conversed as he continued to figure out the woman beside him.

Rich had several incredible dining experiences in upscale restaurants across the country. In his early days of NASCAR, his first trip to the New Hampshire Motor Speedway introduced him to New England seafood. He fell in love with the cuisine. It didn't matter if he picked it up at a local seafood joint or a five-star restaurant. By far, he had never tasted anything better than Chef Jean's lobster clam bake creation.

"She's magnificent! It's ridiculous." Alana

gently touched her napkin to her lips, careful not to blot off the color. "The morning you stopped in to reserve a room, I guaranteed dining here would never be a disappointment."

So far, Rich wasn't disappointed about anything or anyone at the Spring Valley Inn.

Chapter Nine

He would have preferred eating pie, but his wife insisted he speak. Public speaking was not Ryan's forte. He was a man of few words. But two of the things he loved the most, an indescribable love, were his daughters. That love would speak tonight. Daughter number two was getting married. Shauna's eyes sparkled with joy. He stood and clanked his glass with his fork. All attention turned to Ryan.

"Evidently, before we can eat dessert, I've been instructed to speak." He paused, glanced around the table filled with family and friends. His nerves calmed. "Colleen and I want to thank you for being flexible with your holiday schedule. Most don't attend a wedding rehearsal dinner on Thanksgiving, followed by a Christmas Day wedding."

There was no explanation needed. The day after Thanksgiving, the annual Appalachian Christmas Heritage festival kicked off a month-long celebration of the season. Everyone in Spring Valley knew Colleen's year-round Christmas shop, The Old Towne Christmas, was the largest

SANTA'S PROMISING CHRISTMAS

sponsor of the festival. That's how she gained the nickname, 'Mrs. Christmas.'"

"With our schedule, a sane person wouldn't plan a holiday wedding. But I have to admit, we're a Christmas crazy family, and since Christmas brought Shauna and Gabe together, they wanted the holiday to be a central part of their new chapter in life, so here we are." Ryan looked down at his wife and pleaded. "Can we eat dessert now?"

Before Colleen could respond, Abby pushed her seat away from the table and stood. Shauna's eyes widened. Her sister wasn't on the agenda to speak. Abby didn't shy away from public speaking. As an amateur actress, she thrived on it.

"Before dessert, as sister of the bride, I just want to say how grateful I am that I married first." She looked at her husband, Tyler, and continued. "Honey, don't take offense, but there's a reason I rushed you to the alter."

Colleen gave Ryan the side-eye. He looked back, shrugged his shoulders, as if to ask what he was supposed to do.

All the puzzled looks and gestures didn't slow down Abby. "Gran said, back in the day in Appalachia, if your younger sister married first, you had to dance inside a pig trough at the reception." There was a moment of awkward silence. With a straight face, Abby improvised clogging and stomped out a rapid mountain jig. Concluding with a bow, she announced, "Too bad I won't be dancing with pigs, tonight. That would have been a hoot!" Cheers and laughter filled the room.

Shauna joined in the laugher and stood as she told her sister to sit.

"Thank you for fascinating folklore and fancy footwork." She smiled at her sister and continued. "I promise, I won't take long. Since we're all here together as a great big family, we have one more favor to ask." Shauna had a suspicion the answer would be a resounding yes. "As you know, the Giving Tree project brought us together. I thought it would be special if all of us volunteered together to grant a wish."

Gabe added, "The Giving Tree launch isn't until this Sunday and wishes are distributed randomly. Ada normally doesn't break her own rules but agreed to assign us the Haven House women's shelter wish."

One by one, everyone around the table nodded in agreement.

"Perfect, I'll email each of you the list, and together, we'll make another wish come true." Shauna blew a kiss.

One of the things that Alana most enjoyed about Spring Valley, and that made her glad she'd stepped out in faith and took on the inn venture, was her new blended family.

As she sat at the table, sipping wine, she watched friends and family united in love. Even with her challenging schedule, she would make time to help a wish come true for women and children in need.

***

Normally, Rich passed on dessert. Sugar sabotaged his workout efforts. On occasion, he treated himself to a sweet treat—tonight, would be one of those occasions. He calculated he'd consumed enough protein in his lobster dish to stabilize his blood sugar. The first bite of the decadent rich cream lingered on his tongue. He turned to face Alana. His facial expression revealed his thoughts.

Alana's smile turned to a grin, and nibbling her pie, she sat her fork on the plate. "It's wicked awesome!" She realized she let her Boston lingo slip out.

With a nod of agreement, Rich took another bite of Chef Jean's timeless, culinary creation of the Boston Cream Pie. The two-layered golden cake, filled with a rich and velvety pastry cream, was topped with a luscious chocolate icing. "If this is the recipe Gabe followed, it's no wonder he and Shauna fell in love."

From the end of the table Jean shot her younger sister that raised eyebrow, 'I told you so' look. She knew Alana's declaration to swear off sweets would end tonight. Alana couldn't resist the sugar temptation. Watching Rich and Alana engaged in conversation over dinner, Jean was confident Alana's hiatus on her social life might end tonight, as well. Happiness sparkled inside her. Jean's son found love in Spring Valley. Maybe, it was her sister's turn.

For an hour, everything wedding, gift ideas, church, music, and photography filled conversations. The reunion atmosphere offered the opportune time to catch up on the latest news. Ada's husband, J.R., hadn't chatted with Rich for almost two years. J.R. knew the Santa gig was not common knowledge, so he chose another topic. Across the table he inquired, "Are you enjoying retirement? Do you miss the fast-paced crew chief life?

"The first year, I built a new home on the family farm, so that kept me busy. It's taken a while to settle in, but I'm learning to enjoy a slower pace."

"That's an interesting profession. I have a friend in Asheville whose husband was a crew chief in the Air Force," Alana interjected.

"Not that kind of crew chief, my career was in NASCAR," Rich explained.

"Oh!" She smiled, but she never understood that industry, and she was a little perplexed that Rich didn't fit the stereotype.

Rich had seen that weak smile dozens, if not hundreds, of times before. NASCAR is a misunderstood sport. In his younger days, if he encountered negative comments, he felt like he was backed into a corner and had to defend himself. Those days were gone. He never defended the sport he loved—the sport that made him a wealthy man.

"With the racetrack a thirty-minute drive away, when we took over the inn, I was surprised we had regular NASCAR guests." Alana kept the conversation moving. "When I overhear their conversations, it's a foreign language. You'll have to educate me on the sport."

"It would be my pleasure." In his retirement, Rich didn't eat, sleep, and breathe NASCAR, but it was still part of him—part of his heritage.

***

Was she attracted to him or was the third glass of wine responsible for the after-dinner invitation? Rich asked himself as Alana sat next to him on the couch, with crossed legs—one relaxed on top of the other. They were alone. The wedding party had headed to the Mockingbird Coffee House for rehearsal and abandoned them. He didn't feel abandoned.

Gorgeous. He wouldn't lie to himself; he'd admit, physical beauty mattered. But on his recovery journey, he discovered that inner beauty mattered more. Alana was beautiful and had a glow about her that only comes from inner beauty —a radiance that begins in the soul. *Did her story include a spiritual journey?* He wondered.

She was enterprising. The pandemic left its mark on the hospitality industry. He admired her fearless ambition to face challenges head on. He liked a determined woman.

He knew it was true, he'd confess, that more than a few women were captivated by his charm. Likewise, he found women captivating, but in recent years he became very selective in companionship. His best friend was right when he jotted down the list of why Rich needed help in the dating department. He'd have to admit he had fallen for the excuses; he failed at love one too many times and 'a second chance' is a myth. He'd also have to admit his excuses were a safety net to keep him from falling in love—a safeguard for his heart. Maybe, excuses were a crutch, preventing him from living life to its fullest. Maybe, it was time to abandon his safety net excuses. He held cautious optimism.

Chapter Ten

There definitely was no love-hate relationship with her bathroom scales in the past one and a half stress-ridden years. Without a doubt, it was hated. But she knew it was also accountability as the digital screen flashed the unwanted number. The numbers controlled her mood while she dressed to start her day. It was only a number, so why did she let it hijack her frame of mind? She was getting accustomed to her COVID curves. With each passing year she felt powerless over her own body. Gravity seemed to take control. With the shutdown, her metabolism seemed to slow and remained in the proverbial flight-or-fight frazzled stage, hanging on to every calorie needed to cope with tough times. She disliked not being in control of her own body. Fortunately, her free-flowing clothing style helped camouflage the few extra pounds. Or at least, she imagined they did.

Did she also image the connection she felt with Rich last night at the rehearsal dinner? "I don't think I imagined it." She spoke to her reflection in the mirror, as she brushed her hair. She didn't usually wear lipstick to work out. A lip balm would suffice. But, today, she chose the color, Blushing Pout, and filled her lips with a smooth glide. To avoid lipstick on her teeth, she popped her index finger into her mouth, then pulled it out. Admiring her handiwork, she gave herself a little nod. It was the perfect choice to rejuvenate her supple lips, a hint of color for a kissable finish. "You're getting a little ahead of yourself," she mumbled out loud. But kissing crossed her mind last night as she and Rich chatted into the wee hours of the morning. *Stop daydreaming and a get a move on it.*

Alana hadn't seen the number eight on her jean tag in a long time. That was one numeral she missed. A symbol of days gone by. She also missed that forty-something description. Fifty-something just didn't seem to roll off the tongue with ease. Alana was determined that as long as she could put one foot in front of the other, she wasn't going to let a number defeat her. She couldn't change her birth date, but she still had time to reclaim her body and shed those pesky pandemic pounds. Mood would not determine her movements. The pandemic had altered her both inside and out. Neither were welcomed. She packed on a few pounds, but she knew she was not alone. Half the women she met at her new Pilates class had gained weight due to restrictions and the stress that accompanied the disruption in their lives. It was wonderful reuniting with friends to work out, even if it included sweat.

It didn't help that her sister took comfort in stress baking. Evidently, Alana thought, so did everyone else. Supermarkets couldn't keep flour in stock. Alana erroneously blamed her sister, but she knew her own weakness for sourdough bread was the culprit. Things seemed to be returning to normal. Jean was no longer stress-baking. Alana held fast to her exercise routine—Pilates three times a week and jogging on the other days—with the expectation of successful weight loss.

Alana was running late for the early-morning Mockingbird Coffee House pastry run. When they purchased the inn and visited the coffee house for the first time, it only took one bite of Ada's pastries, and Chef Jean decided to feature breakfast pastries in the inn's continental breakfast offered to guests. Jean decided the time she would save baking would free up precious moments for her dinner preparations. Usually, Alana only picked up pastries on her running days, but Jean asked her sis for a favor. She'd decided she would deliver the box of goodies back to the inn, and then she would make her way to the Pilates class. She'd then join her two-person staff to finish decorating the inn.

Alana pulled on her bootcut yoga pants, with the must-have tummy control waist, slipped on her sneakers, and took one last glance in the mirror. She liked the streamline silhouette reflection the pants created—even if it was an illusion. She thought they should change the name from yoga to magic pants—they achieved the impossible feat by taming her curves. She wished she could wear them all day.

With too much exposure to princess movies in her childhood, she also wondered what she'd wish for if the mirror was a magic mirror. That was easy. She'd wish for another evening with Rich.

***

His alarm told him it was time to get out of bed. He wanted to stay lost in the land of nod. Rich wasn't one of those superhuman "short sleepers" who only needed four hours of sleep. One would assume playing Santa was all fun and games, but Rich would beg to differ. It was hard work. He needed sleep. As soon as he opened his eyes, Santa-related activities commanded his thoughts. The tree lighting, the parade, Santa Train Depot, the Dog-Gone pet contest, toys for tots, pics with Santa. Thoughts crowded out the reason for his sleep deprivation. Thoughts of Alana.

He wondered if she thought of him this morning.

He wondered if he should even be considering opening his heart to her.

Then he wondered why he was still lounging in bed, wasting his time, wondering.

He cleared his mind and spoke out loud— words he spoke very morning before rising.

He recited the Serenity Prayer.

"God, grant me the serenity to accept the

things I cannot change, the courage to change the things I can, and the wisdom to know the difference. Living one day at a time, enjoying one moment at a time . . ."

Out of habit, he reached for the sheet, but remembered bed-making would be relinquished to the housekeeping. He'd use the next few minutes to unpack the remaining items in his suitcase. A nester, when he traveled, he liked to settle in as soon as he entered his hotel room. Yesterday afternoon, he'd planned this chore immediately after check-in, but was delayed with an urgent phone call.

Stowed away, adorable teddy bear eyes peeped out of the half-zipped duffle bag. He unzipped the bag and patted the stuffed bear on his plush noggin. He was sure whomever tidied up his room would think it odd. A grown man accompanied by a child's toy? He would have to agree. But this teddy bear was a reminder of a Christmas promise.

The bear originally joined the Ramsey family by way of a wrapped present under the tree. All those years ago, it became five-year-old Courtney's best friend. His sweet daughter named him Teddy.

Eighteen years ago, when Rich sold his house and packed up his daughter's room, he found the beloved bear stashed away in the closet. He remembered the day she asked for his help because the top shelf was out of Courtney's reach.

When Courtney was in middle school, she joined the Beanie Babies craze. It helped that she recruited her dad to hunt for hard-to-find Beanies when he traveled across the country with his racing team. He wasn't the only adult in the toy section because some of his crew joined in the bear hunt when their kids started collecting. Her bed became a kaleidoscope of color with every bear you could imagine. Garcia the Bear, designed with the tie-dye exterior, was Rich's favorite.

She posed each little bear meticulously on her crowded bed. To make room for the plethora of Beanie Babies, she decided to let go of her old stuffed animals she had outgrown—a rite of passage. Teddy was one of the unlucky. His new home became a dark closet where he sat on the top shelf scrunched between the Funshine yellow Care Bear and a redheaded Cabbage Patch Kid doll. Teddy faded into the background of Courtney's life.

Just in case Rich ever saw his daughter again, and if she ever wanted them for her own children, he carefully packed Courtney's Beanie collection and stuffed animals in rubber tubs and stored them all away—except for one.

At home, next to his awards and sports memorabilia in his entertainment room, the love-worn teddy bear took a prominent position on the shelf. Rich wanted a visual reminder of Courtney.

Every Christmas, he placed Teddy under the tree and wished.

This year, sentimental Rich decided Teddy would take a trip with Santa.

Rich glanced around his room at the inn and decided to place Teddy on the fireplace mantle. He looked Teddy straight in the eye, talked to him, as if he expected a response, "I promise, someday, I'll reunite you with your girl."

He'd never admit out loud, but he was convinced Teddy's eyes sparkled.

***

Now, wearing his cold weather running gear, he stepped out in the hallway and jiggled his door to make sure it locked behind him. Simultaneously, Alana's door shut. He looked down the hallway and saw her pretty face. His thoughts resurfaced of the two of them last night, alone, deeply engaged in conversation. He remembered how gorgeous she looked the night before, in the long flowing sassy dress and black high heels. But dressed in yoga pants, crossover shoes, and no makeup—she was naturally beautiful.

"Good morning!"

"Shush!" Alana placed her index finger to closed lips.

The inn felt so much like home, Rich didn't consider other guests may still be snoozing.

She motioned for him to follow. He tip-toed down the stairs.

"Sorry, I didn't mean to shush you. It's an old habit I picked up from the nuns in Catholic school." Alana confessed, "I was shushed on a regular basis by Sister Bernadette."

"I wasn't thinking." That wasn't true; he'd been thinking all morning of Alana, but he just wasn't going to share his thoughts.

Alana kept speaking in a hushed tone. "I've got to pick up pastries from the Mockingbird for the Continental breakfast." She checked out his attire. She was a little jealous of his toned, fit body. "You must start your day with a run."

"The early bird catches the biggest worm." Rich wasn't ready to disclose that running became an intricate part of his recovery journey. He needed that "runners high" energy which lasted hours. "I'm not getting any younger, and I'm praying running will keep my heart healthy."

"This morning I go to my Pilates workout, but I jog three times a week. Maybe we'll cross paths on the trail." She'd contemplated stepping up her jogging routine. This may be the perfect time to take up running, that is, if she didn't embarrass herself.

He was disappointed she didn't invite him to join her, but reminded himself—she did say jog, not run. Maybe, she needed to see his pace before she committed. She didn't know that it wouldn't matter. He would adjust his pace. He'd heard that couples who run together, stay together.

"I'll be on the lookout." Rich looked over to the empty snack and beverage station in the lobby. "No coffee, yet?"

"The early bird may catch the biggest worm,

but he doesn't get coffee this early." She laughed a little.

The corner of his eyes crinkled. He said, in a loud whisper, "Beautiful and funny. And both so early in the morning." He studied her, leaned on the front door with his back, and slowly pushed it open. The antique doorbell jingled. He scrunched his face, expecting another shush. "Sorry. See you."

Alana kept her scrutinizing gemlike eyes locked on Rich, as she carefully walked backwards toward the kitchen to exit through the back door. Her fingers fluttered delicately as she waved goodbye. Flirting? she wondered. Was that what she was doing now? *Absolutely!*

***

There was no one to greet Alana. The Mockingbird Coffee House wasn't officially open for customers. Ada had numerous restaurants and hotels in the area that bought her bakery items wholesale. For convenience, she left the door unlocked for early-morning pick-up.

Cinnamon, gingerbread, and peppermint filled the air. The distinct aroma of Christmas evoked childhood memories spent with her mother and sister standing in line for chocolate drizzled peppermint cannoli from their favorite Italian bakery in Boston. Alana could almost taste the fried pastry shells filled with a sweet creamy filling. They would tote their delectable treats home in a string-tied, white-and-blue box. Nostalgia warmed her heart and triggered cannoli cravings. Once her sugar fast ended, she'd ask Jean to whip up a batch.

Alana heard Ada's voice echoing from the kitchen, chatting with staff. Without permission, because she didn't need it, she opened the swinging door and found Ada boxing up the inn's standard order.

"Good morning!"

"Good morning, to you!" Ada inserted the pastries carefully in the pink bakery box and sealed it with her Mockingbird logo sticker. "You're bright-eyed and bushy-tailed this morning. After the dinner and late-night rehearsal, I ignored my alarm this morning, and J.R. almost had to push me out of bed."

"Walking over here, that burst of cold air smacked me in the face and woke me up."

"Want something warm?" Ada lifted the coffee pot.

"That sounds wonderful! Black." Alana considered this the opportune time to gain intel on Rich. "After everyone left, Rich and I sat out in the lobby and talked for hours."

Ada scrutinized the couple's every move at the rehearsal dinner. She was giddy inside but kept her emotions in check. A stealthy, covert matchmaker should remain composed. She poured two cups of coffee and directed Alana to the bistro table in the corner.

"So, what did you talk about?" Ada nonchalantly stirred in sugar and cream.

"For the amount of time we talked, I think I ended up revealing more than he." She'd liked that about him. He listened. "He's a man of mystery that left me with more questions than answers."

When Ada first met Rich, she too found him evasive, especially compared to other customers who opened up and shared all their secrets—secrets Ada locked up in her heart and threw away the key. She called it—*coffee therapy*.

"What little did you learn?" Ada lifted her mug and sipped.

"Well, let's see. He's retired from NASCAR, which I found fascinating and know nothing about. And if he's retired, he said he was in Spring Valley on business. What business?"

Ada would wait and listen before she replied. Plus, she couldn't squeeze a word in edgewise, even if she wanted.

"He's been married twice. His first wife is deceased, and he said the second marriage was too brief to count—whateva' that means. He has an adult daughter, but he didn't share anything about her. I'm assuming he doesn't have grandkids. If he did, he would have scrolled through endless pictures on his phone, like most grandparents do . . ." Alana noticed Ada leaning in. "Am I talking too fast, I'll slow down."

It tickled Ada that New Englanders were fast talkers. She'd only talk that speedily if she drank ten huge cups of caffeine. Ada nodded and smiled. "Maybe a tad."

"I'm talking too much, anyway. Can you fill in the blank spaces?"

Ada would only share common knowledge. Eventually, Rich shared his story with Ada, and though he didn't ask for discretion, she understood it was not her story to tell. "He's best friends with Ryan, which you probably picked up on that. He's active in his community and church."

"Seriously?" Alana's eyes widened.

"Yes, he is. Does that surprise you?"

"Well, I wouldn't say, surprise. He didn't say or do anything to the contrary."

That little bit of knowledge spoke volumes to Alana—he thought more of others than himself. She'd learned when she moved to the Bible Belt how Sunday morning church attendance was expected. Likewise, a good Catholic attended Mass. Her family considered themselves good Catholics, but she'd let that habit be part of her past. She often thought of going to church, but it stayed way back in her mind. She'd missed it.

Ada decided it was time to end the conversation before she disclosed too much. Alana hadn't mention anything about Father Christmas, so Rich must have decided to keep that a secret. "Oh, my goodness! Look what time it is. I better get a move on." Ada stood and walked to the counter to gather the pink box of goodies.

"Me, too. Jean will be wondering about the pastries." Alana gulped down the last bit of coffee. "I've got a quick Pilates workout, and then we decorate the inn—all before noon."

Ada didn't want her new friend to know she was trying to set her up with Rich. She'd found most didn't like setups, but she was dying to know if Alana was interested. "Before you leave, I have one more question. What do you think of this mystery man?"

"I barely know him, but I like him."

"Plus, handsome!"

"Ada, you're happily married."

"I'm married, but I'm not blind." Ada winked at her.

"You've got that right. He is good-looking!" Alana wondered if that was an advantage or disadvantage? More than once, she'd face the choice of choosing a partner who was either helpful or handsome. She'd never experienced both altruism and attractiveness. That would be nice. But what did she know? It may be a moot point; she didn't have time for romance, and he'd be gone before Christmas.

Alana zipped up her jacket and took the box. "I'm out of here."

"God bless you, girl."

Those words that departed Ada's lips were as natural as breathing. It reminded Alana of a priestly blessing.

Alana pushed open the double swinging door and stepped into the café. Ada's sanctuary. She'd count this as church attendance.

Chapter Eleven

Before noon, their small staff commenced the 'cozy and merry' project. They decked the halls and the rooms' doors with wreaths, placed electric candles in each window, draped roped greenery and hung a festive fruity wreath on the inn's entrance door. To add a wonderful ambience, they strategically placed scented fir and cedarwood fragrance wax candle warmers throughout the inn. The aroma permeated the air, making the inn feel cozy and merry.

"Mission accomplished!" Alana stood with hands on hips admiring their handiwork.

"I think there's something missing." Cydney dropped her head and shoulders in despair. "Where's the tree?"

"The tree is being delivered and set up in the parlor this afternoon." She'd forgotten that this was Cydney's first Christmas at the inn. "You don't have to worry about decorating. After the town's parade and tree lighting, we'll invite guests to help decorate the tree. If that doesn't get everyone in the holiday spirit, nothing will."

"Thank goodness! I'm exhausted, and I

haven't even started housekeeping." Cydney plopped down on the chair.

"Don't get comfortable. We've got a full day ahead."

***

After the two-hour decorating get-together, Alana ran a quick errand downtown to purchase special ornaments for her guests. She'd learned a positive guest experience was vital to satisfaction, a great online review, and the likelihood they would return. To help create a fond memory, guests were gifted an Appalachian folk art hand-crafted, whimsical wooden bird ornament, created by a local wood-carving artist. She'd received an email from the Old Towne Christmas shop to confirm the ornaments had arrived. She welcomed the interruption. She'd be at her desk all afternoon checking in new arrivals, fulfilling any special requests, and working at her computer making sure the Christmas Cookie Pop-Up special event planning was on-track and on-budget.

Spring Valley was Alana's first experience of life in a small town. She liked her new community. She loved the old-fashioned Christmas atmosphere. Vintage lamp posts decorated with illuminated heirloom lantern wreaths tied with red bows and berries lined the street. The brick paved sidewalk reminded her of one of Boston's oldest neighborhoods—the neighborhood of her youth. Boston was a city steeped in U.S. history, and she felt as if she took part in a history lesson every day as she and her sister Jean walked the charming, narrow cobblestone streets, lined with gaslit streetlamps to school, parks, church, restaurants and coffee shops. She'd never imagined, now in their fifties, they would be residing eight hundred miles away from Boston, living in one of the oldest settlements in Tennessee and running an historic inn. History became a part of their lives. Alana decided she liked preserving history and promoting heritage tourism. It gave her a newfound purpose.

She paused at the storefront window to admire one of the entries of the annual Gingerbread Trail contest. She'd watched Jean and Craig labor over it for weeks, but this was her first time to see it in all its glory. Jean created a miniature gingerbread replica of their historic inn. The masterpiece featured frosted and wreath-decked windows and green garland-draped balconies arranged on snowy frosted brick sidewalk with candy streetlamps. It was picture perfect! She didn't expect anything less from her sister.

Alana sauntered in the Old Towne Christmas Shop, slow and leisurely, a total contradiction from her normal hurried pace.

"Looks like someone is in a particularly good mood." Colleen noticed her new friend's carefree smile. "It's been crazy busy. I've been running around here like a chicken with its head cut off just trying to keep up."

"Sounds like a great problem to me." Hoping to avoid discussing the reason for her cheerful mood, Alana walked past the special Santa mailbox drop off and stopped to help a little girl having trouble stuffing the letter in the box. She wished it were that simple, she thought. If only Santa were real, she'd write him a *Dear Santa* letter and beg for help to save the inn from being a casualty of turbulent financial times. If only.

Earlier, she'd considered asking Colleen about Rich, but she'd thought it wasn't fair to ask Colleen since her husband and Rich were best friends.

Colleen walked behind the counter to gather the ornaments. "The rehearsal dinner was perfect! Thank you so much. I think everyone enjoyed themselves. Especially you and Rich."

Alana eyebrows raised. "You're not the first person to notice."

"Let me say, Rich is a great guy. I love him like a brother."

"I will say, he's piqued my interest." She leaned in and whispered, "We stayed up all night talking."

"Aww!" Colleen unwrapped an ornament to show Alana.

"Was that, *aww*, for me or the ornament?"

"You and Rich! But, I must say, Mr. Barnett's ornaments are gorgeous. He's such a craftsman."

With a laugh, Alana inspected the hand-carved bird ornament.

"The guests are going to love these!" Alana noticed a line gathering behind her. "Don't let me keep you. You've got other customers. How much do I owe?"

They finalized the sale. Toting her purchase, Alana waved goodbye. Discontented. She wasn't sure she needed to know more about Rich—she just wanted to know more.

She cautioned herself. She had to focus. She didn't have the time nor the luxury to think about Rich over the next few weeks. She had to prioritize business over romance. Her first priority was a financially solvent inn. A stable relationship wasn't on her Christmas list—it could wait.

***

After spending most of the afternoon finalizing his Santa events, Rich went to the woodworking shop to change into his red suit before the parade. Rich learned at Santa School that it was best not to be seen roaming around in costume before or after a special appearance event. Ryan offered his shop for a changing room.

"In high school, when we raced the streets, you drove like Batman, but I never imagined my best friend would become a superhero." Ryan sat behind his desk and laughed when Rich stepped out of the back room.

"I'm not a superhero."

"Clark Kent walked into a phone booth and changed into Superman. You walked in the workshop, and just like Superman, bam! You changed into Santa. I think that qualifies you as a superhero."

Rich stepped in front of the full-length mirror he'd brought from home.

Ryan shook his head. "I've watched this metamorphosis for five years, but every time, I'm still amazed that no one would ever know it was you."

"That's what I love about it." Rich adjusted his small reading glasses perched on his nose. "I'm a different man when wearing the costume. Past lives are of little importance once I don the suit."

Ryan knew his life-long friend better than anyone. "Rich, you moved beyond your past the day you turned your life over to Christ." He didn't want to get too sappy, but added, "I'm proud to call you my friend."

"Like they say, I'm just turning my pain into purpose. Hopefully, I'm bringing joy into children's lives."

"You're not just bringing joy; you're bringing the true meaning of Christmas." Ryan pointed to Santa's custom-made belt buckle that displayed a nativity scene. It was hand-painted with brilliant colors, so it would stand out.

"It's my little reminder that when all is said and done, Christmas is all about God's gift of love." He pulled an ornament out of his pocket. "This year, I'm giving a little ornament to each child." Rich held the special gift, a tender depiction of Santa Claus kneeling next to baby Jesus in a manger, with a little white lamb at his side. The banner on the bottom read: *That at the name of Jesus every knee should bow.*

"This is incredible, but you'll probably stir up some controversy."

He shrugged his shoulders. "Maybe." Rich slipped it back in his big pocket. "I cleared it with the event planner. I wouldn't mind being known as the Nativity Santa."

Rich had almost an hour before his appearance. He opened Ryan's mini-fridge and grabbed a Diet Coke and plopped down in a chair.

"You're killing me. You're a walking advertisement for Santa."

Ryan grinned as he guzzled his drink.

"I'm going to buy one of those vintage Santa Coca-Cola signs and have you autograph it." He constantly razzed his friend.

"You're so funny. Can we carry on a conversation without any jolly old jokes?"

"Well, it's kind of hard, but I'll try." Ryan stood and retrieved an item from his worktable and handed it to Rich.

"This is exquisite!" Rich held a decorative, hand-carved wooden spoon in his white gloves. The handle scrollwork held symbols of love— hearts, flowers, intertwined knots.

"It's called a love spoon. You're a mountain boy, haven't you seen one before?"

"No, remember, my people weren't whittlers, like yours. We were more into fast cars and making moonshine."

"You got a point there. It's called a love spoon. Money was always tight in the mountains, so instead of an engagement ring, the prospective groom presented a hand-carved wooden spoon."

"It's too large to eat with. Was it just a decorative gift?"

"It demonstrated that the man presenting it was skilled with his hands and would likely be a good provider."

"I'm guessing you gave one to Colleen."

"I did, it's a tradition in our family. Of course, I also gave her an engagement ring."

"Why are you making it? Your daughter is the one getting married."

"It's a gift from Gabe. He tried his hand at whittling but decided that wasn't one of his talents. I finished carving, and Gabe is sanding and applying the stain."

"Shauna will love it!" Rich handed it back to Ryan.

"Speaking of love—" He was anxious to hear what Rich thought of Alana.

Rich interrupted, "I know what you're fishing for, and I'm not biting."

"I just saw some sparks flying and—"

Rich held up his Santa gloved hand to end the conversation.

"Okay, I'll stop. But, I have one more word of advice. Don't go on a date in your Santa suit—it's disturbing." He laughed out loud.

***

Long after the last guests registered and dinner wrapped up, Alana got comfortable on the rocking chair of the second-floor balcony with a cup of cocoa and blanket to warm her legs. Jean and guests of the inn joined her on the prime location to watch the Christmas parade.

She kept glancing over her shoulder to see if Rich would join; after all, he had the coveted Maxwell room with a private balcony entrance. He was a no show. She had no idea where he might be—she hadn't seen him since their sweet little encounter earlier that morning. She surmised he must be about doing whatever business he does.

"We have the best view on Main Street!" Jean rocked back and forth.

"Never pictured you as an old rocking chair granny."

"Look who's talking! You do remember you're the oldest, don't you?"

"You need to be knitting an ugly Christmas sweater." Alana loved teasing her sister.

"I don't knit—I cook."

"Shush! It's starting."

"Don't shush me. It's not like anyone could hear us over all the noise and excitement."

The first sounds of the marching band playing "Deck the Halls" echoed from the other end of Main Street. The children on the balcony clapped in pure delight.

Spring Valley's Christmas parade by night

ushered in the official holiday season. The parade lit up the night featuring marching and dancing bands, antique tractors, beauty queens riding on corvettes, and bedazzled floats sponsored by schools, organizations, and churches who put their heart and soul into the floats. A team of ten mini-horses with decorative antlers won over the hearts of the children. Alana thought it was Americana at its best.

Everyone knew when the parade was about to end with the first sighting of a special appearance from the legendary Santa Claus. His shiny red sleigh rolled smoothly down the parade route pulled by beautiful white horses. The crowd burst into cheers, waving at the jolly old man.

Alana looked at Jean and whispered, so the children wouldn't hear. "For a small-town parade, that costume is incredible. He must have spent a fortune."

"I was just thinking the same thing."

She thought he was a perfect replica, that is, if there was a Santa. A portly, white-bearded man with spectacles was wearing a deep red velvet jacket with faux fur trim, white-fur-cuffed red trousers, a red hat with white fur, and black leather belt and boots. His robust laugh charmed the crowd.

Jean leaned closer to the balcony rail for a better view. "His belt buckle has engravings, but I can't make it out. I wish I had our binoculars."

Alana stood and leaned on the railing. She

caught his eye. She'd swear he was looking directly at her when he waved. She guessed the children on the balcony probably thought the same thing. But there was something more. His eyes lingered. She'd never had the urge to wave at Father Christmas. Tonight, she waved. She gave him a playful smile. Was she caught up in the magic of the season, or was she captivated by a magical Santa?

It was an enchanting evening.

Chapter Twelve

Saturday was a day of smiles and tears, excitement and fears—for the children who heard *"ho, ho, ho"* uttered umpteen times from the holly jolly fellow. What seemed like just another average day for a professional Santa was anything but average for Rich. His first day back at Santa's Train Depot proved to be a miracle—just what he needed to move forward in his life.

He expected the long line of children anxiously awaiting their visit to share their wish list with the wish maker. What he didn't expect was seeing his grandchildren for the very first time! He didn't expect the heartbreaking wish his adorable granddaughter whispered in his ear and the promise he made to keep. He didn't expect his heart would almost beat out of his chest in disbelief that his own Christmas wish was being granted. After all the years of wishing and waiting. It happened. It had to be a divine intervention.

After he left Santa's Train Depot, Rich stopped at Ryan's workshop to change into jeans and a sweater. He previously made arrangements with Ryan, but when Rich arrived, the building was locked. Ryan forgot to leave the key. Rich had no choice but to return to the inn and try to sneak in without being noticed. The innkeepers were unaware they had a special guest at the inn, and he wanted to keep it that way.

He pulled into the reserved parking spot behind the inn. His heart was still racing from the day's surprise. He was taken aback with the encounter and even more surprised that the only person he wanted to share the life-changing experience with was Alana.

When he sneaked in through the back kitchen entrance, he was relieved and shocked it was an empty room. He heard voices in the lobby and dashed up the back stairway to his room. Before he had time to change, the knock sounded at his door.

He looked through the door peephole to find Alana in the hallway, holding fresh towels.

He wanted to keep his Santa identity under wraps. "I just got out of the shower and am changing clothes." He hated to lie, but it was a partial truth. He stared at her through the distorted fisheye lens. Distortion didn't deform her beauty.

"I'm sorry to disturb you. Cydney said you needed towels. I'll just leave these by the door."

"Thank you!" He watched as she walked down the hallway.

Just as he began to shed his red suit, there was another knock at his door.

"Sorry, again." She almost whispered this

time. "Will you be joining us for dinner?"

Rich leaned his back up against the door. His heart raced. Was it still racing from the day's events or knowing she was just on the other side of the door? "Absolutely! I'm famished."

"Tonight, Chef is serving Mediterranean cuisine."

"That's perfect! I love Italian food." He turned and looked through the peephole to take another look. "Are you free after dinner for a stroll downtown?"

As if she knew he was surveying, she looked directly at the peephole. Smiled. "That sounds lovely." She turned and walked down the hallway to the stairwell.

Did he imagine she had a little spring in her step or was it just wishful thinking?

He wrestled with his thoughts. In his mind, he knew he shouldn't share the day's events with Alana. For her to completely understand the miracle, he would have to share his secrets. His past. In all reality, Alana was a stranger. He was a just guest in her inn. Secrets are reserved for best friends. Someone you can trust. Alana seemed trustworthy. He feared, at this point in their relationship, sharing might do more harm than good. But he did find her captivating.

Maybe, soon, he would feel safe enough to surrender his secrets.

***

The scent of basil and garlic and the sound of

conversation filled the dining room. To Alana, it was the smell and sound of success. With dining restrictions officially lifted, guests and local diners were reconnecting with the dining they loved and missed. They missed the cuisine and the homey feeling created by the inn's family-style dining.

Chef Jean wasn't originally a fan of serving family-style. She wasn't a 'pull up a chair, and pass the rolls' kind of chef. She felt it inelegant. She preferred to plate each person's food specifically for them. Chef considered herself an artist, creating individual culinary masterpieces. But, Alana used her power of persuasion and convinced Chef Jean to continue the inn's Southern tradition.

Rich enjoyed the company as he passed the hearty platter of linguine with lobster, shrimp, mussels, and clams covered in a rich tomato lobster sauce. He'd prefer dining alone with Alana, but he enjoyed the warm and inviting atmosphere where strangers became friends. It evoked long ago memories of shared meals with his family and friends. Meals, he hoped someday, would create more memories when he shared around his table with his daughter and grandchildren.

Alana walked in carrying a bountiful basket of warm loaves of bread. And there he was, flashing that million-dollar smile and chatting with new friends around the table. She noticed the empty seat beside him and wondered if he'd saved it for her.

"There she is," Rich announced with a glass

of tea in hand. "I love . . ." He coughed in mid-sentence and took a sip.

Alana sat the basket in the middle of the table, hoping he would finish the sentence.

"Excuse me. I love Italian bread." He flashed her a grin.

A dining-mate chimed in. "Give me a loaf. It's crusty on the outside, soft and fluffy on the inside." He was the first to grab a piece and dip it in a concoction of herbs, garlic, and olive oil. "Perfect!"

Rich stood and pulled out the chair for Alana. "I saved this for you." A Southern gentleman, Rich carried on that tradition. His mamma instilled in him that being a gentleman revolved around respect—respect for yourself and others.

"Thank you!" She was impressed. She liked that custom. Before she sat beside him, she reminded her guests, "I'm dining with everyone tonight, but if you need anything, don't hesitate to ask me or our server, Cydney."

They talked, they laughed, they ate, but most of all, they had an emotional connection. It was comfortable and relaxed conversation with each other and their dining-mates. The soft background music, a sweet sound of the Appalachian dulcimer playing carols, added to the festive atmosphere.

She decided she needed to get back to her hosting duties and excused herself to help serve dessert. They clapped when she returned with a tray of Tiramisu and Chef Jean in tow. Enjoying time spent with guests, the sisters joined the table devouring the creamy ladyfinger dessert.

After the bills were settled, Alana returned to the dining room where she found Rich assisting in clearing the table.

"You're a guest. You shouldn't be working."

"I felt like part of the family, tonight. My mamma had a chore list. My sister set the table, and I cleaned up. Momma lived by a 'divide and conquer' mantra." He stacked the plates on his arm like a professional. "Family members always pitch in."

She teased and did her poor impersonation of the Matthew McConaughey twang, "Alright, alright, alright." She'd wanted to say it since the first day she met Rich and heard his accent.

Rich threw a napkin her way. "That was really bad. McConaughey would be embarrassed for you."

"A Bostonian has trouble with Southern accents. What did you expect?"

"It's a little more like this . . ."

Rich nailed the celebrity's one-of-a-kind voice.

Alana was a little embarrassed, starstruck, and weak-kneed.

**

Rich took the steps two at a time to retrieve his jacket for their evening stroll. As he came back down the stairs, Alana shot him a smile. He stopped mid-way when he got a call on his iPhone. He had one reason not to answer—she was waiting at the bottom of the stairs. He had several reasons to pick up—it was Friday night, holidays can be the most challenging and stressful time of the year for sobriety, it was Ainsley's first 6 months of recovery. He knew the highs and lows of holidays. He also knew he needed to answer. "Hello, Ainsley. Give me a moment."

His eyes met hers. Eyes begging for forgiveness, he told Alana he needed to take the call. He didn't know how long he would be away, so he suggested they take their stroll another night.

At first, she was so bewildered, all she could do was nod her head. Alana watched as he wandered back upstairs to his room, phone in hand, talking to someone called Ainsley.

She'd thought her mind would be filled with images of Rich and her enjoying a romantic moonlit walk down the snow dusted sidewalk. Now, she had the name Ainsley stuck in her head.

She reminded herself she was the innkeeper; he was her guest. It was against policies for employees to fraternize with guests. From this point forward, she needed to keep their relationship strictly business.

Chapter Thirteen

As promised, Rich pulled into the church parking lot at nine forty-five to meet Ryan and Collen for worship service. Rich saw them standing beside their vehicle. He parked in the empty space beside them.

Before Rich got out of his truck, Ryan opened the passenger door and poked his head inside.

"I'm so sorry, I forgot to leave the key last night."

"Beggars can't be choosers." Rich didn't want to give him a hard time.

"Did anyone spy you sneaking in the inn?"

"No, Santa's stealthy. I think I'm good."

"I promise, I'll have a duplicate made tomorrow and drop it by."

They walked down the sidewalk to the entrance, greeting other church goers.

Colleen inquired, "I thought maybe you'd have a guest with you this morning."

With a smile, Rich held the door. "So, you're in on the matchmaking service, too?"

Colleen noticed her question remained unanswered.

Rich had planned to invite Alana to join him, but last night's call cancelled their walk and his church invitation.

Music signaled the start of the service. A praise team accompanied by keyboards and electric and acoustic guitars began worship with a new arrangement of the old Christmas classic, "Joy to the World - Unspeakable Joy."

That's what he'd experienced—unspeakable joy. Rich sat in the sanctuary, reflecting on his journey. Before he turned his life over to Christ, he'd never considered himself much of a religious man. Religion skipped a generation with his parents. Rich's dad wanted nothing to do with sanctimonious hypocrites in the church. As a child, what Rich knew of God, he'd learned from his Bible-believing grandparents. Disappointed that their own son took a path that led him away from church, Granny and Papaw held out hope for their grandson. Rich remembered Granny telling him she prayed that one day he would see the light.

Granny warned anyone who would listen that *alcohol was the Devil's tool*. Rich thought his dad must have owned the Devil's toolbox. He'd swore he would never follow in his father's footsteps, but like his dad, Rich became an alcoholic.

A co-worker invited Rich to attend a recovery program at a local church. Rich thanked God every day that he took that first step which led him to his new life. Granny's prayer was answered

—he saw the Light.

Forty-eight hours ago, his fervent prayer was answered—he got a glimpse of his daughter and his grandchildren. For the first time in his life, he saw his grandchildren.

Through his recovery journey, he'd found peace with things he couldn't change.

He'd lived with unanswered prayers.

He'd prayed when he didn't know what to say.

He'd prayed his daughter would forgive him for things she couldn't forget.

He'd held on to the power and promises of prayer.

Today, there was no other place he would rather be than in a worship service. His heart overflowed with gratitude for God's blessings. For answered prayers. He recalled words of the psalmist: *What a beautiful thing, God, to give thanks, to sing an anthem to you.* He'd been faithful to his church. God remained forever-faithful to him.

The service ran a few minutes late. It would be a miracle if he didn't get caught, but he'd have to rush back to the inn, sneak in the back door and change for his Santa duties at the Dog Gone Christmas Pet contest. Families loved to flood their Instagram feed with their fur babies' pictures with Saint Nick. He always allowed extra time for prepping the pets. Pet pics were more stressful than kids. He'd keep plenty of treats in his pockets.

He wondered if his grandchildren had a dog.

Chapter Fourteen

O n her Sunday morning walk, Alana attempted, without success, to block out the sudden interruption that ended a splendid evening. Last night, after Rich chose to talk with Ainsley, instead of her, she'd decided to keep things strictly business. It made sense in her mind, but not in her heart. Never before in her life had she fallen for a guy so quickly. Why, she questioned silently, had she fallen so hard?

The vibration of her phone interrupted her contemplation, and she took a break, sat on a bench, and answered. Jean was on the other end. "Why aren't you answering your phone?"

"Excuse me, but I'm talking to you." Jean's frustration convinced her to quickly double-check to see if she had missed calls. She had.

"Cydney tried calling to let you know she wouldn't be in until noon." Jean's voice rose.

"Sorry, I just saw where I missed her calls." Alana confessed. "I'll be back in a few minutes, dressed and reporting for duty before you have a panic attack."

"It's too late for that."

The pandemic came and left. Guests

returned but all of her staff didn't. They were still understaffed. She'd thought she could manage a small inn with her eyes closed. She soon found out, she needed to do it with both eyes open.

At least, she thought, crisis management forced her to keep her mind on business.

She showered and dressed in record time. When she walked in the kitchen, Jean stood in her usual early morning spot, staring at the whiteboard as she reviewed Sunday's schedule. They abandoned their bickering sisters' routine and busied themselves with setting up the Continental Breakfast table, chatted with guests, suggested holiday events, and assisted with checkout. Cydney arrived after noon for housekeeping services.

Crisis averted, the sisters took a few minutes to grab a quick bite before Jean began to prep for dinner.

Agitated, Jean thought. Alana seldom if ever let a little thing like an employee running late upset her. "Are you mad at me for interrupting your morning walk?"

Alana plopped down two Diet Coke cans and began pouring into glasses.

"No, that was no big deal."

"Well, something is bothering you. You've been sighing with those long deep breaths all morning."

"I don't want to talk about it."

"You know you can't get rid of me. I'll keep

asking, so you might as well talk."

More often than not, Alana admired that characteristic of her sister. Jean was relentless. She was her built-in best friend. Her protector. Her confidant. Even though they fought like cats and dogs growing up, they became best friends. She needed to talk it over with her best friend.

In defeat, Alana held up a napkin and waved. "You win! I raise the white flag."

"That's what sisters are for." Jean lifted her glass of Coke and took a sip. "Before you start, does this have anything to do with your downtown stroll with Rich last night?"

"Bingo!"

"And I had such high hopes for you two." Jean wrinkled a frown.

"There was no stroll. Just as we were ready to walk out the door, he received a call from some woman named Ainsley. He apologized, said he needed to take the call, didn't know how long he would be on the phone, and we would take a stroll another night."

"I'm sorry. I wonder who's the mystery woman. Is that his daughter?"

"No, her name is Courtney."

Jean placed her hand on her cheek, carefully evaluating the information. "He didn't give you any explanation?"

"No, and it happened so fast, I was dumbstruck. All I did was nod in agreement and watch as he walked back to his room."

"Wow! I've never seen you dumbstruck. I'm sorry I missed it." Jean hoped levity would help.

"I blame those mesmerizing smoky gray eyes of his. They begged forgiveness, and all I could do was nod." She shook her head in disbelief.

"Man, he's good."

"Doesn't matter. I reminded myself that it's against policy for employees to fraternize with guests. From this point forward, it's strictly business."

"I must have missed that staff meeting." Jean knew there was no such policy. "Maybe the Biltmore included that code of behavior in their employee handbook, but we didn't."

"Well, we should."

"No, we shouldn't. Since I'm married to my stove, meeting a guest may be my only chance for romance."

"What about the produce guy? I've noticed he's been lingering, and it's not just haggling over the price of zucchini." She took a drink

"First off, he has a name—it's Arrow."

Alana laughed in her glass. "You're kidding me, right? His name is Arrow, like shot from a bow?

"I didn't name him." She smirked. "It's a Southern name. I thought it sounded masculine and strong." She continued, "Second, you're diverting the topic of conversation." Jean didn't admit out loud that she had her eye on the produce guy. She'd save that story for another talkfest.

"I'm the queen of diversion."

"I have a few words of wisdom to convey." Jean shot out her finger at her sister. "Don't make a snap decision based on this one incident. For all you know, Ainsley could have been a nurse, calling to give an update on his poor ailing mother in a nursing home." Jean hoped that provided some food for thought. "You have a tendency to overthink. Just focus on having a little fun."

"I admit, I'm also the queen of overthinking."

"Add drama queen to the list."

"I didn't realize we were cataloging."

The black Labrador racing through the back kitchen door cut their conversation off and brought Alana reprieve. Gabe was a few steps trailing his dog, Big Papi.

Jean quickly transitioned from sister to chef reprimanding her son, "Get that dog out of my kitchen. The Health Department will shut us down." She loved her son and his dog, but the dog was not welcome in her place of business.

The harsh tone stopped Big Papi in his tracks. He looked at her with a tilted-head puppy dog expression. He was confused. Big Papi had a new residence with Gabe out on the mountain top but couldn't understand why he wasn't allowed in his old home. He loved living out in the woods, chasing squirrels, but he'd lived here before this strange woman with a funny hat. Banned, he waited for Gabe outside in the courtyard.

"Sorry, Mom. He got away from me." He gave Jean a big hug and kiss on the cheek, then greeted his Aunt Alana the same.

"Just wanted to dop by and say hello before I picked up Shauna and thc twins."

"I see you made a Dunks run and didn't think of your poor mother."

Gabe held a coveted Dunkin' Donuts coffee cup. "That's how Big Papi escaped. I wouldn't drop my cup to grab him with both hands."

"I'd kill for some coffee regular." Jean had coffee in her veins.

"Sorry, next time, I promise." He sipped on his favorite brew.

"What do you guys have going on this afternoon?"

"We're taking Paige, Bryce, and Big Papi for a visit and pictures with Santa."

"That's so sweet." Alana loved Shauna's twin niece and nephew. She'd seen them from time-to-time at their grandmother's shop.

"The first Christmas we met, since the twins don't have a dog because their dad is allergic, they borrowed Big Papi for their pics with Santa. It's become a tradition. This year, they're dressing Big Papi in a costume and entering him in the Dog Gone Christmas Pet contest."

"Maybe that's why he ran from you. He doesn't like to wear clothes."

"He loves it! It's a Grinch inspired costume. They're certain he'll win first place."

"Text pics."

"I will. By the way, did you get the email with the wish list for the women's shelter?"

"Yes, I'm making extra cookie decorating kits for the children." Jean was relieved with the easy task that didn't require leaving her kitchen.

"Rich and I have been assigned the gift buying task. Shauna included the age and gender of the children, so now all we have to do is shop." She walked over to the refrigerator for another drink.

"That shouldn't be a chore for you since you love to shop." Jean teased.

"I do, but I don't have a lot of experience buying for children. I'm thrilled they included ideas."

"Have you set a shopping date with Rich?" Gabe raised his eyebrows.

"It's not a date," Alana corrected her nephew. "It's wish granting shopping."

"Whatever you say." Gabe winked at his beloved aunt. "I hate to cut this visit short," Gabe looked at the wall clock, "but I need to be on my way."

Before he left, Jean needed to relay some disappointing news. "Wait a minute, I'm glad you stopped by. I wanted to tell you in person that your grandparents are not going to be able to make it to the wedding."

"I thought that might be the case. I warned Shauna not to get her hopes up. She was looking forward to meeting them."

"Mother and Father are both in their eighties, and with their medical conditions, they have an increased risk for severe illness. Their physician advised them not to travel."

"That makes me sad, but I totally understand."

Always the problem solver, Alana suggested, "We could set up an iPad in the balcony and do a live stream on FaceTime."

"That would be perfect! I remember seeing that option on our wedding photographer's website. We'll just add it to our package."

"Mother and Father will pay the extra cost."

"That's not a problem. I'm sure they have someone on their staff to help with technology; we can make it happen." Big Papi barked, impatiently reminding him they had other places to go, squirrels to chase, and pictures to take. "I'm out of here." Gabe walked toward the back door. "Love you two."

"Love you, too." They chimed in together.

With julienned vegetables on the dinner menu, Jean pulled out carrots, squash, and zucchini from the cooler and began her vegetable wash.

Before Craig arrived to assist with evening meal prep, Alana took the opportunity to broach a sensitive subject with Jean.

"Since we're on the subject of Mother, Father, and finances, they've offered to gift us money for the inn—no strings attached."

With her back to her sister, Jean looked over her shoulder and gave Alana that, don't go there look.

Alana went there.

"I think you're just being stubborn."

Jean carried the vegetables to the counter, selected a chef knife and proceeded to cut her first slice of the zucchini. "You know very well, during my unplanned pregnancy, they tried to force adoption. When I chose to raise Gabe on my own, they withdrew their financial support."

Alana watched her sister's frustration grow as the knife hit the chopping board harder and harder with each slice.

"You don't have to remind me. I was there. I let you move into my apartment. Remember, I was your birthing coach. When Gabe was born, I felt like his second mom."

"I swore I would never take a dime of their money."

"I didn't take that oath. It doesn't bother me."

Jean yanked a carrot, quickly peeled and trimmed the top, cut a thin slice for a stable base, turned it flat side down and thinly sliced lengthwise, stacked the slices and cut lengthwise again. All in a matter of seconds. Alana thought she needed to stay clear of her sister's razor-sharp knife.

She appealed to Jean's nostalgia. "But when

Gabe was a toddler, their hearts softened, and they accepted you and Gabe back into the family dynasty. Everything's fine."

"Yes, and I welcomed their love but not their loot." Thin uniform strips of colorful vegetables piled on the cutting board.

"I don't know why we're having this discussion. Before we bought the inn, we agreed not to go to our parents for financing."

"That was before the pandemic. We're in a different financial world. So far, we've been fortunate, and our doors are still open. We're recovering, but I don't know how long we can keep this up." Trying to win her sister over, Alana added another justification. "You do know we will eventually inherit the majority of their estate."

Jean's eyes welled with tears. She never forgot the abandonment she felt when her parents turned her away—when she needed them most. Gabe was two years old when she abandoned her resentment and chose forgiveness. She loved her parents. They loved her. They loved Gabe. She didn't want to think about death, let alone talk about it.

"Alana, there are times I lay awake at night, preparing myself for the inevitable. I know Mother and Father will not live forever. We all have that unavoidable appointment, but do we need to discuss it this very moment?" Her eyes begged Alana to wrap up the conversation.

"Let's re-evaluate after the holidays and then

decide."

"I promise, I'll consider."

Resigned, Alana shrugged, and walked over to hug her sister. "If you put your knife down, I'll give you a hug."

Jean placed her knife on the countertop, dabbed away her tears with her apron, and hugged Alana. She wasn't comfortable with the conversation. It caused her to question the oath she made as a teenager. Jean's parents spoke a different love language than hers. Theirs was giving. Hers was spending quality time with the people she loved. She wondered, and feared, if over the years they felt unforgiven and dejected when she refused their financial assistance. If she accepted their gift now, she asked herself, would they grow even closer and love better? They only had so many days or years left on this earth. She still had time. She didn't want to live with regrets.

Alana pointed to a carrot. "May I have one?" She waited for Jean's nod of approval before she snatched and crunched.

"Are we good?"

"Yes, we're good. But if you decide to solve the world's problem in my kitchen again, you'll be sitting out in the courtyard with Big Papi." She wagged her knife in a threatening way.

"I'm gone!" She strolled out of the kitchen, then popped her head back in. "Since I have your permission to fraternize with guests, I'll be out fraternizing."

Chapter Fifteen

Rich loved the sweet silence of an early morning run. He tried not to think when he ran. He used running to find solitude, peace, and time for silent prayer. Today, he kept thinking of the word, yes.

With the parade, the first Santa Train Depot event, and the Dog Gone contest all declared huge successes, Rich felt comfortable with his holiday appearance schedule. An overbooked calendar was always his greatest challenge. He didn't want to overpromise. He hated to say "no" to last-minute requests but had to allow time for unscheduled visits to hospitals and nursing homes to spread cheer and brighten someone's day. Even the oldest patients enjoyed a visit from the big guy from the North Pole. He'd say "yes" to those things that brought joy.

He thought about the day when he'd said "yes" to Santa School on a whim when he came across that old plastic Santa decoration of his childhood—the shabby jolly old Saint Nick with a painted twinkle in his eye that always gave the family great joy. Nostalgia led him to google *How to become a professional Santa*? Obedience guided his decision to register for the school.

He'd become bored in retirement and wrestled with a new plan for his life. He'd prayed for a new purpose. He knew the historical Saint Nicholas was a man known for his charity and generosity as he went from home-to-home giving gifts. But something clicked when he read one particular sentence on the Santa School homepage: *Saint Nicholas's actions were celebrating the love of the Savior.* Taking on the role of an infamous character seemed daunting. But fueled by faith, Rich decided this adventure was the answer to his prayers and said "yes" to God. He'd found a new track to share and celebrate the love of his Savior. He was convinced that was a decision instrumental in finding, and hopefully, reuniting him with his daughter.

He thought of Alana. The one person with whom he wanted to share his incredible news, but hesitated. He shook his head as if to expel the thought. He'd share his past story dozens, no hundreds, of times at recovery meetings. He questioned why he held such fears and reservations to tell her. He reminded himself that he'd traded in his fears for hope decades ago and said "yes" to himself. He'd share his story with Alana.

He would pass the Mockingbird Coffee House on the way back to the inn. He decided he'd stop for a chocolate milk recovery drink.

Surprised to find the place empty, he

SANTA'S PROMISING CHRISTMAS 124

wondered if it was too early for business and Ada had failed to lock up the previous night. Singing echoing from the kitchen and the sweet, yeasty aroma of fresh baked bread dispelled that concern. He walked in the kitchen and found Ada pulling a hot tray out of the oven.

"Anybody home?"

Totally preoccupied on her baking, Ada was unaware of the man who stood in her kitchen. His voice startled her. She let out a whoop, "Woo-whee! Dagnabbit!" She almost threw the pan.

"You scared me half to death." Embarrassed and a little annoyed, she came close to losing a morning's worth of baking. She sat the pan on the counter. She declared, "That's enough to make a preacher's wife curse."

Throwing back his head, Rich laughed freely. "I'm so sorry, Ada. I didn't mean to frighten you."

That laugh made Ada grin. Her nerves calmed. "The jingle sleigh bells on the front door usually alerts me; you must have sneaked in like a burglar."

Rich put his finger to his lips and secretly said, "Santa gets practice sneaking around homes at night putting presents under the tree." He noticed no other staff in the kitchen. "Are you all by your lonesome this morning?"

She pointed to the wall clock that read six-fifteen. "Staff don't arrive until seven-ish. We don't open until nine. I leave the front door open for early morning pick-up for wholesale customers."

"I'm sorry. I was out for a run and forgot about the early hour." He started to push the swinging door open to make a quick get-away. "I'll get out of your hair."

Ada never turned anyone away. Plus, she needed an update on her matchmaking. "No, you don't. You can keep me company for a few minutes. I need to sit a spell to calm my nerves." She pointed for him to have a seat at the bistro table in the corner. "Coffee?"

"Do you have any chocolate milk?"

Puzzled, she asked, "Really?"

"It's a good recovery drink after a long run."

Ada grabbed the grown man a kid-sized bottle of chocolate milk, selected a grown-up mug for herself, poured a cup of coffee, and joined him at the table.

Ada added milk and sugar, watching as he took his first gulp. "So, how's Alana?"

Rich almost spit out his drink. "You don't waste any time, do you?"

"You're not getting any younger. You don't have any time to waste, do you?" She gave him a saintly grin and picked up her coffee mug.

"You got a point." He murmured. Ada had a way of making people feel comfortable enough to spill the beans. She'd known him for years but didn't know his recovery story. He felt he could trust Ada. Rich started spilling.

In the limited time he had before the staff

arrived, he told Ada the abbreviated story of his past, his daughter leaving, his recovery, and then filled Ada in on the last few eventful days. He proceeded to tell her that Alana intrigued him, and yes, he had undeniable feelings for her but feared rejection. He moved on to the greatest news—getting a glimpse of his long-lost daughter and his grandchildren and the indescribable joy and gratitude he felt. But, he'd held both excitement and trepidation for his next steps to reconciliation.

Listening to the story filled with highs and lows told in rapid succession, Ada experienced roller coaster emotions—the full range, from sadness to joy. Ada worried this might be more than her nerves could take. Especially, the first thing in the morning. She also thought he was a skillful secret keeper. All the times she served him coffee, she never knew.

Ada was so happy for Rich; she wanted to hoot and holler and dance a jig. But an employee walked in the door. She thought it best to curtail her excitement. Across the table, she reached over and laid her hand on his and patted his hand, like the touch of a loving grandmother. She was overjoyed. Her beaming smile conveyed her feelings. "The good Lord works in mysterious ways. He brought you this far, He won't abandon you now." She squeezed his hand. "I'll make you a promise. I'll keep praying if you promise to keep hoping."

Emboldened, he jogged back to the inn to find the innkeeper.

***

Chef Jean was in the kitchen at the first flush of morning. A stand mixer needed repaired. Normally, she would've contacted a service facility, but her budget didn't allow for such luxuries. In kitchen emergencies, she'd repaired broken appliances over her career, but she stationed her iPad beside her on a YouTube tutorial to refresh her memory—which, lately, needed a lot of refreshing. She successfully completed the task just in time to chat with her produce vendor, Arrow, then made a quick trip to the Mockingbird to pick up pastries for breakfast.

While driving, she passed Rich jogging back toward the inn. She smiled and waved. He waved back.

"Wouldn't it be lovely," she thought, "if Rich became Alana's boyfriend?" That word, *boyfriend*, sounded too juvenile. She needed a more mature noun. She thought. Partner was too generic. Friend, too casual. Lover gave the impression of a salacious affair. She remembered what her mother called their boyfriends—admirers. It had an elegant Victorian-era flair. If Alana had an admirer, things would change.

She'd adjusted to their new sister adventure. The move to Spring Valley to be close to her son and purchase the inn was a good change.

Jean always wanted the best for her

beautiful, talented, successful sister, but Alana had her fair share of bad boyfriends and a failed marriage. It would be wonderful, she thought, if Alana had a second chance at love.

Jean decided if romance knocked on her door, and if she answered, instead of referring to him as her admirer, she would speak romantic French, *mon amour*. My love.

The wish for a second chance had even crossed her own mind a few times when she chatted with Arrow.

Mon amour. She should add that to her Christmas list.

Chapter Sixteen

S he was summoned. As expected, Jean found Alana behind her desk, phone cradled on her shoulder, while simultaneously talking and typing a reservation on her computer. Alana gave a hard nod toward the empty chair facing her desk, and recognizing the command, Jean took a seat, wondering why she was called to meet her sister out front. Alana usually popped in the kitchen for impromptu hotel management meetings.

Alana ended the call, sat back, and smiled. "Do you want the good news or bad news first?"

"Please, start with the good."

"The pop-up Christmas cookie shop event is sold out!"

"That's incredible! Just a few days ago, you were concerned with slow registration. I wonder what happened." Jean began to worry if she'd baked enough cookies for the decorating kits. "So, what's the bad news?"

"Evidently, someone said they spotted Santa entering the inn, rumors spread like wildfire that the jolly old man may pop in at the pop-up." Alana threw her hands up. "I have no idea how this ridiculous gossip spreads."

"Did you tell them that Santa would not make an appearance?"

"I thought about it, but the pop-up event adds so much revenue, I decided I would try for a last-minute booking."

"Good luck with that. I'm sure you have to book months in advance."

"Thanks for being Negative Nancy."

Jean rolled her eyes. "You pride yourself in crisis management. You'll fix the problem. Just let me know how many kits we'll need." Jean stood and turned toward the kitchen door.

"So that's how you're going to help, by walking away?" She lowered her voice and glanced around to make sure guests wouldn't hear.

Alana hadn't realized someone was listening in on their conversation.

"I didn't hear you enter." Miffed at herself for bantering with her sister in the lobby, Alana smiled a courteous, innkeeper smile.

"So I'm told. Evidently, I walk softly." Rich walked closer to her desk. "I think I can help with your problem."

"Unless you know a professional Santa, I don't see how."

Without a word, Rich motioned for her to follow him.

Jean watched as Alana, without questioning, followed him up the steps. Jean smiled and thought he must have magic in those eyes. She also thought it was awkward seeing her sister follow a man to his room. She giggled remembering their fraternizing conversation. She could hardly wait to hear what her sister had to report. She shook her head and went back to the kitchen to inventory cookies. Jean had a suspicion she would be baking more gingerbread.

***

When Alana entered his room, the air smelled of a rich, woody aroma. A masculine combination of musk and citrus essence. She recognized it as his signature scent. Warm and robust. She could inhale this all day. She dreaded when housekeeping cleaned the room leaving no trace of the previous guest—as if he were never there. She reprimanded herself for blindly following Rich to his room—*total unprofessionalism*. She didn't know what came over her.

Puzzled, she watched as Rich opened the closet door to reveal unexpected contents. Sandwiched between designer sweaters and running gear, the red suit hung in the middle of the neatly organized wardrobe. The fat suit crowded the ensemble. A white wig and beard set, classic hat with white pom-pom, and belt lay on the top shelf. Tall, fur-trimmed, wide-top, black boots stood beside his running shoes.

He wasn't just an intriguing, handsome man. He was Santa! She couldn't contain her laughter.

"You've got to be kidding—you're Santa?" She knew that sounded childish. But she'd have to admit her inner child never stopped believing.

"I'm not the real Santa. I'm just his helper."

"I have so many questions." She sat on the cushioned bench at the end of the bed. "So, this is why you're in town on business?"

Rich grinned and nodded up and down.

"That was you, wasn't it, in the parade?" She realized that's why she was captivated by the magical Santa in the horse-drawn carriage.

He nodded.

"So, it actually happened. It's not just a rumor that someone saw Santa sneaking into the inn?"

Rich kept nodding as she interrogated him.

"Can you respond with words?"

Rick nodded, smiled, and spoke, "I arranged to change at Ryan's woodworking shop, but he forgot to leave a key. We were instructed at Santa School to not be seen roaming around town in costume—"

She interrupted, "Wait. Did you say Santa School? There's really a school? Did you walk across a stage and receive a diploma?" She wished he'd stop grinning at her.

He laughed and nodded again. He closed the closet door, hoping to focus her attention.

"Go on."

"Anyways, I got locked out after the event at the train depot. I waited until late to return to the inn. I entered through the back kitchen door and sneaked up the back stairway. I thought I made it without being seen, but evidently, someone saw me. I feel awful."

"You should feel awful," she declared. "Are you going to be a good little Santa and help me out?" She pouted her lips.

His scheduled was crammed, but Rich reminded himself that just a few hours earlier, he resolved to say "yes" to things that brought joy. "Yes, but full disclosure, I can't bake."

"That's not a problem. The cookies are pre-baked. The kids are only decorating," she assured him. "I just need you to pop in for a personal appearance, take a selfie, and you can dash away, dash away, dash away all!" Her eyes danced with laughter.

"Oh, like I've never heard that before." He grinned, crossed his arms, and leaned against the closet. "When do I need to show up?"

"Wednesday, Thursday and Friday at one-fifteen."

"I'll be there."

The man who stood before her had not been punctual for the rehearsal dinner. She wondered if when dressed in the red suit, would he be on time? She stood and walked toward the door. "Promise me, you'll arrive at one-fifteen."

"I promise." He crossed his heart.

The door closed behind her, leaving Rich to cope with a mixture of relief and apprehension. He let out a deep breath, one little secret revealed— one more to go.

Chapter Seventeen

Wednesday morning, after hitting the snooze button one too many times, Alana settled for a quick home Pilates session. She unrolled her mat on the bedroom floor and got in a fifteen-minute workout. She didn't push herself as hard as her instructor would have, but the combo of planks, lunges, and squats worked up a good sweat before showering and dressing for her busy day. She'd be setting up for the pop-up cookie shop, but before that event began, there were her day-to-day tasks of an innkeeper that took precedence. She longed for the day when she'd hire an assistant.

Alana hurried downstairs, tidying up and inspecting as she went along her way. She made a mental note to tell Cydney to dust and wax the furniture in the upstairs hallway. The gorgeous antique pieces were a perfect choice for the historic inn, telling a story of the inn's past while creating an elegant ambiance. However, they required regular maintenance which seemed to have been overlooked. Alana reminded herself to not be so 'to-the-point' with Cydney. There were a few instances when Alana feared Cydney would not be returning to work. Alana didn't mean to hurt her feelings, but before Cydney became accustomed to Alana's personality, she wilted like a flower during her on-the-job training. Alana learned being blunt and straightforward might be understood as business as usual up North but not down South. Cydney worked full-time but the workload required more personnel. Alana also longed for the day when she'd hire additional housekeeping staff.

Before eleven, Chef Jean and Craig finished putting the cookie kits together. Each holiday themed bakery box came complete with three icing colors and ten assorted cookie characters—including Chef Jean's award winning, gingerbread men in cinnamon brown sugar.

They carried the kits to the dining room where Alana made final preparations for the cookie decorating pop-up shop. She arranged the tables as decorating stations and covered them with red and white snowflake tablecloths, strategically placing the individual cookie kits to give each child enough elbow room. She also laid out the festive waterproof aprons to protect the littles' clothes and handwipes to clean up the mess. All the fun songs needed to fill the air with Christmas cheer played over the sound system, giving the inn a fun and festive atmosphere.

Jean came back for a final inspection. She stood beside her sister and studied the setup. "This looks fantastic. But, I wish we could have used the kitchen as a classroom. The mini-holiday workshop we offered at the culinary institute was one of my favorite classes I taught."

"Me, too. I bet the kids felt like little chefs in that professional setting. Our kitchen is just too small for the number we have registered. I hope we can handle that many excited kids."

"It will be fine," Jean assured.

"Who are you and what have you done with my sister?"

"That's what holidays are all about—family, friends, food, and fun."

"You use a lot of French phrases, but I don't think *laissez faire* is in your vocabulary."

"You know me better than that. You've been watching too many cooking shows where Hollywood portrays chefs as cruel, mean taskmasters. I admit I'm detail-oriented and maybe come across as a little bossy in the kitchen, but I can have fun with kids." Jean looked at Alana for agreement. "*Oui?*"

"*Oui, oui!*" Failing miserably at her French accent, Alana changed the subject and reminded the crew of their duties. "Jean and Craig are in charge of instruction, while Cydney and I will assist in piping the icing. I'm sure we can get the adults to help." She looked directly at Cydney. "From time-to-time, you may be on your own if I'm needed at the front desk."

Jean glanced and saw Cydney looking like a deer in headlights.

"Don't worry. We've got everything under control." Jean gave them the thumbs up.

"One more thing, Santa is popping in at one-fifteen. He'll only be here for a few minutes, but I expect pandemonium. So, be prepared."

"I'm just glad he squeezed us in his schedule. It's a Christmas miracle!" Jean was on a roll. "I can see the headlines, Santa Saves Sister's Inn."

Alana smiled and rolled her eyes. "Meet back here no later than twelve forty-five."

They parted with Jean, Craig and Cydney darting back to the kitchen, and Alana moving toward the front desk.

Alana caught a glimpse of herself in the hallway mirror and frowned. She slipped into the powder room to primp. She freshened her lipstick and ran her fingers through her messy pixie cut to fluff it up. She'd need product to get the perfect piecey look but remembered it wouldn't matter—she'd be wearing an elf hat. She blotted her lips and hurried back to the lobby.

When the first child arrived, everyone was ready. Alana and Cydney wearing elf costumes greeted their young guests. Cydney opted to wear black leggings and her own knit top, with a green elf inspired red ruffled apron embellished with tiny bells and a matching hat. Alana, always guilty of making a fashion statement, wore a sassy green elf dress, black belt, candy cane stripped leggings, ankle boots, and a curved peaked elf hat. As expected, Chef Jean, always the consummate professional, strolled in from the kitchen wearing her chef's uniform, but celebrating the holidays, broke tradition and wore a red chef hat. Trailing behind her, Craig wore crazy baggy chef pants with a colorful chili pepper Santa hat design and a matching skull cap.

With the number of oohs, aahs, and giggles, Alana was convinced the pop-up Christmas cookie shop was moving toward being known as the most fun holiday destination for kids in Spring Valley. It was impossible to stop grinning, witnessing their enjoyment and watching moms posting on social media. Alana knew the event was well on its way to exceeding expectations. Each child managed to slip the adorable holiday apron's loop over their head and with a little assistance, tied the back string around their waist. Their eyes almost popped out of their heads when Chef Jean handed each child their own red paper chef hat. Jean loved inspiring little chefs in training. Excitement was building, anticipating a visit from the jolly old man. Alana found herself thinking she too could hardly wait for his arrival.

True to his promise, Santa made his grand entrance through the lobby at one-fifteen, dressed in his glorious red suit, ringing sleigh bells, and singing, "Rudolph the Red-Nosed Reindeer." The children immediately joined in the spontaneous sing-a-long. Alana thought it was a wonderful way to engage the children. Walking from table to table, he greeted each child by name. Not realizing their aprons had nametags, the miniature chefs beamed from the recognition. For the adults in the room, watching the look of surprise on their faces was priceless. It added to the magic of Saint Nicolas. He stayed in character and gave Alana that irresistible smile and wiggled his eyebrows. His eyes sparkled behind his reading glasses. But what Alana didn't know was his eyes almost popped out of his head seeing her decked out in that sassy elf dress.

Decorating to the holiday music in the background, they piped and frosted snowmen, trees, and gingerbread men masterpieces. Making memories, each child held their cookie showpiece and took a selfie with Santa.

In the middle of having fun, Alana noticed as Santa pulled out his cell phone, read the text message, and announced to the kids, "Just got a text from my top elf. There's an emergency at the toyshop. I'll be right back." He excused himself and disappeared to the kitchen. Upon his return he declared, "Ho, ho, ho, no need to worry! The elves have everything under control. All the toys will be ready for Christmas!"

Cydney, an elf for the day, joined in the fun and began clapping and excitedly jumping up and down in celebration. The kids started cheering.

Alana, wondering if she had anything to worry about, leaned in and whispered to Chef Jean, "I wonder if that call was from elf Ainsley."

Without saying a word, Jean, raised an

eyebrow and slightly curled her lips to a weak smile to let Alana know this wasn't the time or place for theorizing. A little miffed and embarrassed with herself, Alana went about her elf duties. She'd erase that thought from her mind and stop sabotaging what was turning out to be a delightful afternoon.

With his busy schedule, Rich stayed longer than she anticipated. She had no doubt he enjoyed being in the same room with her. Even though he was unrecognizable in costume, there was still no mistaking his distinguishable, smiling eyes and stolen glances.

After the last selfie, Santa gifted each child an ornament, a tender depiction of Santa Claus kneeling next to baby Jesus in a manger with a little white lamb at his side. It warmed her heart.

They were all making memories. She recalled the saying, *Santa enters through the heart*. She'd remember this day as the day she opened her heart to him.

Chapter Eighteen

After leaving the pop-up cookie workshop, Rich made a surprise visit to the Children's Hospital where he had the privilege to hold a newborn for a Baby's First Christmas picture with Santa. Parents, fearing their baby born with a heart defect wouldn't see her first Christmas, received an answer to prayer when the surgeon was able to repair her heart. He'd always treasure those tender, sweet moments.

He needed a long nap before his evening commitments. He returned to the coveted Maxwell room, closed the blinds, plugged his phone in the charger, placed his watch on the nightstand, and carried his pajamas to the bath. Once he shed his Santa costume and fat suit and washed the spirit gum off his face, he dressed in his red pajamas. He had to start choosing a color besides red, he told himself.

He stacked the multitude of pillows on the chair beside the bed which proved to be a balancing act. Why, he questioned with a shaking head, did decorators think every bed needed a half-dozen throw pillows? He pulled down the fluffy duvet and fell into bed.

He closed his eyes. His body relaxed. His mind worried.

He worried how to find where Courtney and his grandchildren were living.

He worried if things were moving too fast with Alana.

He worried about Ainsley's struggles in recovery.

He decided to stop worrying and start praying. He prayed himself to sleep.

He drifted in and out of consciousness. The music from the next room woke him. New guests must have arrived, he thought. Evidently, they were not aware Santa was napping in the next room. He wouldn't complain. Noise meant revenue for the inn.

He decided to wear a navy, ragg wool crewneck sweater and jeans. He'd always liked the red and white snowflake Fair Isle pattern, once a classic and now an "It" item. He pushed his sleeves up revealing his toned arms and Tissot watch.

Rich shut the door behind him and took the back stairway, hoping he would find Alana in the kitchen.

Thanks to Alana and Chef Jean making final preparations for the evening dining for the guests, they were deep in conversation and work. Before they knew he was coming down the stairs, he had the good fortune of eavesdropping. Hearing their glowing review of the Santa appearance made him smile. He'd remembered how miffed Alana was earlier when she didn't know he was standing close by and listening in on their conversation, so he decided to clear his throat.

She looked up and smiled. "Did you not notice the "Employee's Only" sign on the stairway door?" She teased.

"I did, bu—"

Jean interrupted, "After today's fantastic workshop, he can use any stairway he wants. Heck, you have my permission to slide down the banister!"

Rich let out a laugh. "I'll stick to the stairs."

"Will you not be joining us for dinner?" Alana presumed she knew the answer.

"No, I have another commitment this evening." He looked Alana in the eyes. "Got a minute?"

"Give me a sec, and I'm all yours." She turned to finish filling the breadbasket.

He liked the sound of that—*I'm all yours*.

Chef Jean took that as a signal he needed privacy. She announced she needed something from the butler's pantry and made herself scarce.

"Okay." Intrigued, Alana turned to face him. "What's on your mind?"

"I have a houseboat on Lady Lake. I have a free night tomorrow and wondered if you would like to join me for dinner on my boat."

"Well, you're just full of surprises. It just so happens, I'm free, as well. I've heard the lake is beautiful. I would love to go."

He loved her gleaming smile with her kissable lips.

"Do I need to bring anything?"

"No, just your beautiful self." He walked toward the door and paused. "I'll meet you in the lobby tomorrow night at six."

"Perfect." She closed the door and watched from the kitchen as he walked to his truck. She didn't have to wait a full twenty-four hours. She'd see him tomorrow at the cookie workshop.

She wondered what commitment he was running off to this evening and why he didn't feel the need to share.

She wondered when her heart would stop racing.

She also wondered why she was acting like a nervous high school girl being asked on a date. She laughed, wondering if it had anything to do with being asked out by Santa.

Alana turned and found her sister staring at her with a Cheshire Cat grin on her face.

"Thanks for scurrying off and giving us a little privacy."

"My pleasure." With raised eyebrows she commanded, "Spill."

"I'm going on a date tomorrow night. He's taking me to his houseboat on the lake for dinner." She put her elbow on the counter and cupped her face. "I've never been to a lake this time of year in this climate. What will I wear?"

Jean shook her head. "You just got asked out

on a date by the most interesting man in the world, and your first comment is, 'What will I wear?'"

"You sound like a Dos Equis beer commercial." She tilted her head in dreamy thought. "I have to admit, they both rock that silver fox look." She reached in the breadbasket, broke a piece off, and nibbled on some bread. "It's getting cold. I'll need to dress warm."

"The way things were heating up in the kitchen, I have a suspicion he'll keep you warm."

Alana picked up an oven mitt and threw it at her sister. Jean caught it mid-air and tossed it back.

"We have a dining room full of guests." She pointed at the oven. "Put that mitt to work. Later, you can spend all night in front of the mirror choosing the perfect lake apparel." Alana was always the fashionista, Jean thought. She knew whatever her sister wore would be modern, classy, and effortlessly chic. She'd seen the way Rich looked at her sister. Alana didn't need to dress to impress—he was already impressed.

***

Yes, I would love to.

That was the answer Rich had hoped for. With his mind on Alana, he drove to the town of Bristol to his recovery meeting.

He'd thought dinner on his houseboat would be perfect for their first date. He'd always prefer the privacy the lake provided. The lake community gossip didn't bother him; speculating was a sport with them. He loved the unique, close-knit water neighborhood where everyone looked out for each other. The community welcomed him with open arms.

Growing up, Rich didn't live far from Lady Lake. It was a popular destination for locals and tourists, a hidden gem tucked away in the mountains. He'd occasionally go swimming and fishing with his, buddies but his dad didn't have any interest in family fun at the lake. Besides, boats were an expensive hobby, and his dad poured all of his extra money in his race cars. While living in North Carolina, after a family tragedy, Rich made frequent trips home to visit the family. On one trip, he met up with an old friend, who was now a doctor, who invited him to spend some quite lake time for some fishing and drinking.

At a difficult time in Doc Leonard's life, Doc found tranquility on the lake and decided to say good-bye to his land-lover life and trade it in for full-time serenity houseboat living. Rich smiled, remembering when Doc found the love of his life at Lady Lake. His prescription for Rich was to spend time floating on the lake for his mental well-being. Rich did just what the doctor ordered which proved to be a cure for his heavyheartedness. In the course of time, he bought a 60-foot houseboat and secured a premium slip at the marina, with a backdrop of the Cherokee National Forest and a gorgeous sunrise view. He'd even imagined, after retirement, he'd consider full-time houseboat living. Eventually, on his recovery journey, Rich substituted Diet Coke for beer. The lake became his favorite vacation destination—his sanctuary.

He hoped his safe harbor would be the ideal environment for sharing secrets.

Chapter Nineteen

Rich sat waiting in the lobby of the Spring Valley Inn. A few weeks ago, he thought it was just a place for convenient lodging. It wasn't—it was a crossroads.

The leather wingback chair gave a refined atmosphere to the décor and a comfortable, cozy invitation for a guest to sit back and relax. He sat back but didn't relax. This time, Alana was not just a charming innkeeper, she was his date.

He felt somewhat bizarre, not in a freakish way, but an unexpected, foreign emotion—a promising feeling.

It was only a night out on the lake, he reminded himself. He was probably making a big deal over a first date. He failed to ask if she experienced motion sickness. He'd have to remember to ask her before they left. A queasy stomach would be disastrous.

He heard footsteps on the stairway. She came into view at the middle landing. He'd expected his heart to begin racing, just as it did every time he saw her, but he also felt his knees turning to water. A gentleman stands when a lady approaches, but she made standing almost impossible. Nervous energy willed him to his feet. A smiled tugged at his lips.

She hadn't been on a boat in a few years. She hadn't been on a date in two years, she reminded herself. She'd tried several ensembles before settling on skinny blue jeans, a retro denim blouse with a long, cozy fleece-lined, hooded jacket and brown leather booties with a low heel and rubber soles. When she saw him, her knees wobbled a little. She reached for the handrail and supported herself as her hand smoothly glided down the banister.

"I hope my boots are okay." She lifted her foot for a quick inspection. "I don't have any deck shoes; I'm counting on the rubber soles to keep me from slipping."

Boating etiquette was not his concern. Rich was not about to put a damper on the evening by telling her that black soles are not welcome on a boat because they leave marks on white decks. He'd welcome her wearing combat boots.

"You're perfect!"

So, she thought, he thinks I'm perfect.

"Let's use the kitchen door to the back parking lot, so I can let Jean known that I'm leaving."

He followed her into the kitchen and watched as she said her goodbye to Jean. Sweet, he thought, how their sister bond was strong. He also thought it was somewhat intimating. He felt extra pressure assuming he had to impress her sister, as well. Why did he assume anything? He stopped thinking. Why set himself up for disappointment? It was time to do away with expectations. He'd made the decision years ago to turn his life and will over to the care of God—every aspect, even dating.

"Be home by midnight," Jean teased while wagging a wooden spoon.

At least, Rich thought she was teasing.

"You're not my mother—just a bossy sister. Besides, I haven't had a curfew in over forty years."

He held the kitchen door open for Alana, glanced back, and winked at Jean. "See you!"

"Enjoy your evening!" She winked back.

As Rich walked around to open the door, Alana complimented his vintage ride, "I like your truck."

"Thanks, you can call her Betsy."

As she waited for him to get behind the wheel, she wondered if everyone in the South named their vehicles. "I've never known anyone who named their car. Is that a thing around here?"

"Absolutely, Betsy has been in my family for almost eighty years. She deserves special recognition." He backed out of the parking space and pulled out onto the road. "And yes, it's a Southern thing and a car thing. I know all the names of my friends' cars, too."

Caught up in their comfortable, relaxed, and sometimes flirty conversation, the minutes flew, and by the time they arrived at their exit ramp, dusk had turned dark.

"Oh, no! There must be an accident." Seeing the brake lights of cars backed up on the exit ramp alarmed Alana.

"I forgot to warn you. This is traffic for the Bristol Speedway in Lights." Rich slowed his truck to a crawl in the designated through lane. "That's why I chose tonight. This is bad, but Friday and Saturday nights are horribly congested."

"So, this is Bristol?"

"This is Bristol, baby!" He burst out.

From her startled look, he realized his declaration was the first time she'd heard that expression. He laughed out loud. She wasn't laughing.

"You've got a lot to learn about NASCAR."

"How about starting with this?" She pointed to the cars they passed. "I've seen advertisements for the event, but I never imagined it caused traffic jams."

"You've got to get out more."

"Let me remind you, my first holiday in Spring Valley, the shutdown cancelled everything. Last year, I still wasn't crazy about getting out and about. This is my first full-blown holiday celebration."

"Speedway in Lights is an incredible holiday light spectacular, self-driving tour, stretching over a 4-mile trek through three million lights. At the end of the tour, fans get a chance to take a lap as your car comes out onto Turn #4 on the track.

It's a fan's dream come true. It has extraordinarily steep banking. It's exhilarating and terrifying. As slow as they go, they get the feeling like the vehicle is about to tip over. But believe me, it's nothing compared to racing at 200mph, but when else would a fan get to take a lap?"

"Is that a rhetorical question?"

He smiled and kept telling her about the event as he impatiently drove a snail's pace. He was waiting to hear her reaction when she saw the speedway.

"They have every light display you could imagine. In the center of the speedway is the Christmas Village with carnival rides and shops. You can toast marshmallows and warm up by the fire and have your picture made with Santa."

"Oh, my gosh!" She interrupted. "It's amazing. It looks like a coliseum." She leaned lower near the windshield for a better view. The glow from the light show lit up the sky. "I never imagined it being this—" She searched for the best adjectives.

"Monstrous." He completed her sentence. "You should see it in daylight."

"I'll have to," she agreed, "if you'll be my tour guide."

He looked forward to introducing her to his world.

"Absolutely! You hit the nail on the head with the coliseum description. One of its nicknames is The Last Great Coliseum. It seats

160,000 cheering fans in stadium-like seating."

"Sounds like it's gladiators in fast cars."

"Fast, furious, and loud. Insanely loud."

She could almost feel his adrenaline pumping as he introduced her to his sport. "Tell me more about this event."

"It's sponsored by Bristol Speedway Children's Charities. A classmate of mine from high school, Claudia, directs the organization. It's raised over $19 million dollars since its inception with the sole purpose of distributing the funds to qualified local children's organizations. It's made a tremendous difference in the lives of children in our local community."

"I'm surprised you aren't the Santa of choice."

"I've filled in a couple of times during Santa emergencies, but it's all consuming. I wouldn't have time for any other appearances. But, I do donate everything I make from appearances to the charity."

She took a mental note that she needed to add *charitable* to the pros and cons decision making relationship list. Thus far, his pros were outweighing the cons.

Chapter Twenty

After dinner they sipped coffee while the boat gently rocked. A peaceful breeze whispered through the trees. It was a perfect evening. The moon poured shimmering gold, spreading a glow over the lake as the water lapped against the shore. The air was cool with the scent of pine. Together, stargazing was an amazing experience. Alana thought she'd found paradise nestled in the Tennessee hills. Winter had chased away sounds of nature in the forest surrounding the lake. Only the deep hooting of a great horned owl cut through the darkness.

Rich looked over at Alana. "Aren't you going to answer?"

"Answer what?"

"The owl, he's asking you, 'Who cooks for you, who cooks for you all?'"

"I didn't get that. Are you an owl whisperer?"

"Listen closely to the rhythm, he'll ask again."

On cue, the owl called, "Hoo hoo hoohoo, hoo hoo hoohooahh?"

She listened carefully. "I heard it!"

"My papaw taught me to listen to bird calls.

He said the Cherokee Indians that once inhabited these hills claimed a single hoot signifies death, two hoots imply success, three hoots mean women would marry into the family, four hoots signify unrest, and five hoots signify travel."

"I wasn't counting, which one did we hear?"

He grinned. "It was three hoots. According to the folklore, a woman will soon marry into the Ramsey family."

"You'll have to invite me to your wedding," she teased.

"I certainly will. You'll be the first to know." He wasn't teasing.

His response surprised Alana, sensing there was truth in his words. She purposely and slowly drew the mug to her mouth, allowing for silence. *Why would a simple, flirty comment compel her to think of wedding bells?* she wondered, staring at the lake, careful not to look into his eyes. She'd thought wedding bells after fifty was a hopeless pipe dream. Maybe a happily ever after, after fifty, really does happen, or maybe, she considered, she was looking forward to seeing Rich in formal wear at her nephew's Christmas day wedding. Either one was a pleasant thought.

"Was moving to Spring Valley everything you'd hoped it would be?"

Shifting to a more comfortable position on the loveseat, she tucked one leg under the other and turned to face him. "I don't know if I really had any great expectations. Jean and I decided at this juncture in life, we needed a sister adventure. So, a small inn, a small town, and a big adventure in semi-retirement sounded great. It's definitely had challenges with the shutdown, but hopefully, we'll pull through. Overall, it's been promising." She'd left out her thoughts on the promising idea of a second chance at love.

It was bizarre and enchanting going on a date with a professional Santa. She wondered what caused him to wake up one day and decide to enroll in Santa School. Alana knew very little about Rich. She knew he'd retired as a crew chief from NASCAR, and during the holidays he'd dress in a red suit spreading cheer. But she hadn't known why he chose to leave his career and why he clammed up on the subject of family.

"You seem awfully young to retire. From what little I know of NASCAR, involvement in the sport is like a religion. Why walk away?"

"I love racing and it's been good to me, but it was my time to retire. These days a crew chief has to be a rocket scientist with a fancy degree hanging on your wall. I broke into racing almost three decades ago. I was a blue-collar machinist who had a lot of grease under my fingernails, loved racing, and thought I had the skill set to succeed in motorsport. I was lucky and among the last of a breed that only attended technical school with most of my training being hands-on at the racetrack." He paused the conversation to retrieve the coffee pot to warm their drinks.

"Did you follow in your father's footsteps?"

"I did. Dad was a mechanic and had a passion for stock car racing. But, he wasn't too happy when I chose the racetrack over a degree. He only made it so far without a formal education and wanted more for me."

"Sounds like you made the right choice."

Since she was a motorsport novice, Rich decided to give her the abbreviated version of his career. "It was all about right timing. I started before the advancements in computer technology when you could break into racing if you were a machinist." She leaned in with interest, but he knew he was speaking a foreign language. "Early in my career, I had an opportunity to work with a racing team in North Carolina. As I worked my way up to crew chief and the sport became driven by technology and more complex, I was savvy enough to employ engineering graduates as team members. We were fortunate to win a few championships."

"When did you decide to go to Santa School?"

"The short answer is after I retired. The long answer involves my life story that led me to that point." In spite of his discomfort and fear of rejection, Rich knew it was time to share everything with Alana. "You want to hear it?" He nervously rubbed the back of his neck.

"You have my undivided attention." She smiled to assure him. She sat her mug on the side table, zipped up her hoodie, and put her hands in her warm pockets. She'd wondered what secrets this man held, and she was about to find out. It made her stomach feel queasy.

He was quiet for a moment, took a deep breath and began, "If you have questions, jump in at any time."

"I will," she said quietly. "I'm not going anywhere."

Those words comforted him—for the moment. He wondered if she would feel the same in a few minutes.

"The Christmas my first wife Rachael and I celebrated our twentieth wedding anniversary was the same year we held her funeral." He looked out over the lake remembering. "We'd had a rocky relationship, mainly due to me being a high-functioning alcoholic. I could work all day without any issues, but as soon as I left work, I had a beer in my hand. I'd promised Rachael we would go Christmas shopping for our daughter, Courtney, but I came home wasted, and we got into a big fight. Courtney was sixteen. Her mom called and told Courtney to stay the night with her friend. Then Rachael left without me." He paused. The sound of waves softly lapping on the shore and faint voices in the distant filled the silence.

Alana dreaded what she guessed would be the rest of the story.

"I dozed off in my Lazy Boy recliner, only to be awakened a few hours later by banging on my door. I stumbled to the door and was greeted by a somber deputy and Sheriff Steve. I knew the sheriff, but from the looks on their faces, I was certain it wasn't a social call." He stopped for a second to look in Alana eyes. She'd remained silent but listened. Searching her bright jewel toned eyes he saw no panic, just calm composure. His attention drifted back to the lake.

"I'm sure the sheriff recognized that familiar glazed-over look in my eyes. I remember the house being dark, except for the glow of the lights from the Christmas tree. Sheriff Steve switched on a light, took me by the elbow, and led me back to my chair where he proceeded to tell me that Rachael had been killed in a car accident." Rich paused, vividly remembering he was glad he was seated; otherwise, his knees would have buckled under the weight of the overwhelming news. He hadn't had time to sleep off his latest bender and was still groggy, but he'd managed to hear what they were saying. He'd asked questions, but he hadn't fully comprehended. He remembered he'd tried to tame his trembling hands by gripping the arms of the chair.

He continued, "The sheriff asked about Courtney and offered to do what he hated the most about his job—death notification, especially when it involved a teenage girl whose life would be torn apart in an instant. I knew I was in no condition, so I did the cowardly thing and took him up on his offer." Rich took another deep breath thinking of Courtney. "We had our problems, but I loved my wife. She'd said that I had a hard way of showing it. We'd always told each other 'I love you' before we left the house. Since we'd just fought, I was mad and too tanked to utter those words when she left. She was furious and probably wouldn't have received it, anyway. But the last words I remember her saying when she slammed the door were 'Don't expect a present from me.' The irony is, on the way to the mall, she was hit head-on by a drunk driver. They both died instantly." The thought haunted him that a drunk ran her out of the house, and another drunk got behind the wheel, ran straight into her, and took her life.

Heartache filled Alana's heart and eyes but not for herself. Heartache for Rich and the unimaginable grief and guilt he carried.

He finished. "My daughter blamed me for her mother's death. And to be honest, I blamed myself, too. I wasn't the drunk driver that killed her, but I could have been. I'd been behind a wheel many times too drunk to drive. For all intents and purposes, her mother's death and my addiction destroyed our father-daughter relationship. Two years later, Courtney left home, swearing she would never step foot in my home again, and she hasn't," he said wearily. "She's texted occasionally on a burner phone to let me know she's okay, but that's been our only communication."

"Oh, Rich, I'm so sorry," Alana whispered.

"That was over two decades ago," he

continued. "But by the grace of God, a co-worker invited me to attend a recovery meeting at his church, and that's the day I stepped out of my own denial and walked into God's grace. I've been twenty years sober, getting right with God, myself, and others."

She remembered the night he refused wine at dinner and opted for tea. She remembered the night they talked into the wee hours of the morning. She remembered too, telling Jean she had the feeling he was holding secrets. After he revealed his Santa secret, she still had the feeling he was hiding something. Now she understood. His story was too personal, and she had to gain his trust before he would invite her into his past.

She took her hands out of her pockets and reached for his. "Thank you for trusting me enough to share your story. I can't imagine the grief and pain you must have been through. And your daughter. What a horrible thought to lose your daughter's love." She saw the hurt in his face. "I'm sorry, I shouldn't have said that."

He lifted her hands to his lips and kissed gently. "No, you're right. Until tonight, I've never heard someone say it out loud. I lost her love, but I've never stopped loving her." His vision blurred as he blinked away the tears. They sat in silence for a few moments, gazing at the stars. Thinking he needed to add a little levity, he asked, "You want to hear the rest of the story? It's about the jolly old man in the red suit."

With a small laugh, she pleaded, "Please, tell me the ho, ho, ho story."

He let out a big laugh and shared his childhood memory of the shabby plastic Santa and of how boredom set in during retirement. He openly shared how the risk of relapse ran high for him during holidays and how he prayed for a new, fulfilling purpose in his life, which led him to the decision of playing the role of Santa. He shared how it was an answer to his prayers, and he'd found a new way to celebrate and share the love of the Savior.

He saved the best part for last.

"I've been dying to tell you the good news." Rich stated with hope. "Every year my only Christmas wish is that I would see my daughter. Last week, at the Santa Train Depot, she was standing in line with her two children for pictures with Santa."

Alana gasped, "Oh my goodness! What did you do?" She studied him with awestruck eyes.

"Honestly, I just about had a heart attack. I was in costume, so there was no way she would've recognized me. She looked the same, just more mature. I would have recognized her anywhere. When the kids—my grandkids, sat on my lap and whispered their wish list, my heart melted."

"So, did you tell her?"

"No, something inside me told me to *wait*. I've learned to listen to that still, small voice even when every ounce in my body wants to do the opposite."

"What are you going to do?"

"I'm going to wait. Now that I know she must live in the area, I'm praying our paths will cross again. I had my helper give them free tickets to Santa's Breakfast. I watched and when the kids showed Courtney the tickets, she turned and mouthed, 'thank-you.'" Rich teared up reliving the moment his granddaughter ran back and gave him another heartwarming hug. And when they walked away, they turned and waved goodbye. He, in turn, waved, winked, and prayed. He added, "She provided their names for the reservation list. I took that as a good sign. You're not going to believe what the kids names are." He sat with a big grin on his face.

"Are you going to make me guess?"

"I would, but we would be here all night. My granddaughter's name is Grace and my grandson's name is Chance."

She gave him a puzzled look. "I don't get it."

"I see God's power and hope in their names. The significance of forgiveness and a second chance." He shrugged his shoulders and smiled. "Just sayin'."

"Wow!" She shivered. "I don't know if that's what sent a shiver up my spine or if I'm getting too cold."

The outdoor deck heater was set on low, but the temperature had drastically dropped. Rich wrapped a throw blanket around her and left his arm draped over her shoulders. Alana nuzzled closer and looked up at him with tenderness and compassion. He needed nothing more to draw her into an embrace. He pressed his lips to hers.

He lifted his head away for a moment. "Should I have asked first?" He whispered.

Alana's answer was another kiss, laying her lips gently on his. Lingering and savoring each moment.

Rich thought her lips were not the first lips he'd kissed, but he hoped they would be the only lips he'd be kissing the rest of his life.

All of a sudden, Alana felt queasy. She'd experienced lovesick butterflies in her stomach before, but not like this. Of all the times to have motion sickness, she worried. She'd been thinking about kissing him for days.

When a second wave of nausea washed over her, Alana pulled away.

Rich had seen that look too many times. He could kick himself for failing to ask if she'd ever experienced motion sickness.

"Alana, are you okay?"

She stilled herself and took a deep breath. "I think I'll be okay. I just feel a little nauseous."

"Just let my ego think it was the kiss."

She wanted to laugh but couldn't. But in her distress, she still thought, *he could kiss!* For now, she decided she would keep that little secret to herself. "Dang it! This isn't how I envisioned the evening. Just give me a minute, I'll be alright."

Her face told another story. "We need to get you on solid ground. Let me get you a Dramamine, ginger ale, and some crackers, and we'll walk back to the truck." Rich quickly grabbed the items and returned, only to make the boat rock harder. Her eyes widened as panic spread over her face. "Breathe slowly." He took her by the arm and helped her off the boat.

She'd stopped protesting. The dock swayed. She was sure she'd lose her dinner if she didn't get to the parking lot—soon. Rich held her close, careful so they both wouldn't end up swimming in the cold, dark water. Close enough to kiss, she thought. If only she'd taken Dramamine earlier, they'd still been on the boat wrapped in each other's arms.

He helped her in and started the engine to warm the truck. She closed her eyes and sat back, resting her head on the truck's bench seat. She wondered why he hadn't put the vehicle in gear.

"Are we not leaving?"

"I thought we'd sit here for a few minutes and let you sip your drink and nibble on your crackers." He leaned over and gently touched her brow. "Let me know when you feel the world's stopped moving, and we'll drive back to the inn."

"I'm fine." She lied. She wasn't fine. She was sick and embarrassed. "What about the boat? We left everything out."

"Don't worry. Like I said, we look out for each other in our lake community. I'll call the dock owner and ask him to close up the boat," he assured her. "Just breathe slow breaths, relax, and think pleasant thoughts."

Watching her closely, her lips slowly formed a smile. Her eyes still shut, she reached over searching for him, and his strong fingers closed over her delicate hand.

Holding her hand, emotions surged through his body. They sat in silence. There were no words, but their intertwined fingers were communicating trust, empathy, and love.

He'd revealed his big secret. He'd feared judgement and rejection, but she graciously gave compassion and acceptance.

He followed his own advice. He breathed slowly, relaxed, and thought pleasant thoughts.

Chapter Twenty-One

By midnight, Alana felt she'd managed to calm her queasy stomach. In her pajamas she sat alone in her bed, sipping on ginger ale. She reminded herself that unfortunate things happen, right? Even with Rich's revelations, she decided, she'd felt it was an enchanting evening. If only her stomach hadn't sabotaged their date. They'd planned a shopping trip, which didn't require motion sickness meds. She held great expectations for their official second date.

Life seemed harder, she thought as she nibbled on a cracker. When you're young, she frowned, everything looked so easy for adults. Dating after fifty—definitely, wasn't easier.

She heard a faint knock on her door. Jean popped her head in the room and saw that Alana was awake, sitting up in her bed. "I thought I heard you sneaking in. And before midnight. I was just teasing about the midnight curfew." Before Alana warned her against it, she climbed up and made herself comfortable at the foot of the bed.

"Don't rock the bed!" Alana waved her off the bed. "I'm seasick."

Jean got a closer look and saw all the color

had drained from Alana's face. She was as pale as a ghost. Jean sat on the chair beside the bed and put her hand to her mouth to hold back the laughter. She wasn't successful.

"Don't you dare." Alana threw a throw pillow at her sister. "It's not funny!"

"You've got to admit, it's a little funny." She giggled. "Did you hurl?"

"No, but I came really close." She rubbed her stomach. "I feel so much better now."

"So, was the date a total disaster?"

" No, it was incredible. We really connected."

"Tell me, what it's like dating Santa?" She teased.

"Let me just say, Santa can kiss!" Alana's eyes danced.

Jean clapped in approval.

"Keep the noise down; remember we live in a hotel. We've got close neighbors."

"Tell. Me. Everything."

"Grab a tissue and fasten your seatbelt. It's quite a story."

Jean settled in the soft, cozy chair and listened as Alana shared all she'd learned about Rich. And to Alana's relief, she discovered the mysterious calls that Rich kept receiving were from someone he was sponsoring. And Ainsley was a man as their recovery group does not allow someone to sponsor the opposite sex.

She told Jean everything.

"That's quite a story." Jean dabbed her

eyes when Alana told her about Rich seeing his grandchildren for the first time. "What was going through your mind when he revealed he was a recovering alcoholic? Did you see any red flags?"

"To be honest, at first, when he talked about being a functioning alcoholic, I had concerns, but as he revealed more of his story, I was blown away that he felt comfortable enough to trust me with his deepest struggles and emotions." Alana took a sip of her soda. "Remember, he's been twenty years sober."

"I've had friends in recovery, but there's always that possibility of relapse. Are you sure you're ready to dive into a relationship with that possibility looming?" Jean felt their lifelong bond of sisterhood gave her the permission to ask probing questions.

Irritated, Alana frowned. "I'm not that innocent schoolgirl, sharing secrets with my sister. Good grief, there's always a possibility of something bad happening. I didn't think my husband would cheat on me, and I'd end up a divorcee, but I survived, didn't I?"

"Yes, you not only survived, but you also thrived. I just don't want you to jump too quickly in a relationship."

"Excuse me, but weren't you the one encouraging me?"

"I said just have fun and see what happens. From what you've told me, you're falling for him."

"Whether I'm falling for him or not, tonight

I saw a man who was willing to bare his soul. His flaws. His struggles. I saw a man who overcame a tragedy, had the courage to change, and daily strives to be a better man. He's kind, gentle, generous, and appears to be a godly man. I find that very attractive."

Jean added a little levity. "You forgot to add to the list, he's Santa."

"That too! Just think about it. I don't know if it was a form of penitence, but he decided playing the role of Santa gave him the opportunity to share the love of Christ. I think I'd like to date a guy like that, wouldn't you?"

"We can't both date him. That would be weird." Jean scooted out of the chair and kissed her sister on the forehead. "It's almost one o'clock. We can solve your love life in the morning. Sweet dreams."

That's what Alana was hoping for—sweet dreams.

⁂

He sat in a rocking chair on the balcony, the east side of Main Street, coffee mug in hand. Well past midnight, the town slept. He didn't. An awakening to an encounter of his Maker's presence in his life left him pondering.

Just a few days earlier, he'd toured Main Street in a horse-drawn carriage dressed as Santa. He had a different perspective sitting high above the charming little town. Draped in twinkling lights, the cobblestone streets and eighteen-century structures held stories of the past. He'd read of presidents traveling through the Appalachian Mountains on the Great Stage Road and lodging in town. Chances were, he sat and rocked on a balcony where presidents and dignitaries once came together, discussing the future of the country. His gaze drew upward. He counted six illuminated church steeples, spires lighting up the darkness of the night sky, a reassuring sign of hope and God's presence in our lives. He'd wondered if the townsfolk had ever considered renaming the street to Church Street. His mind journeyed into the past, wondering how God worked among the early settlers of Spring Valley when religion brought an awakening to their sleepy little town. He also felt connections to the prayers of the faithful offered in their sanctuaries and marveled at how those prayers are still echoing down through history.

God was at work today. Life was changing for him at breakneck speed. He'd never imagined he would find his daughter in Spring Valley, let alone discover he had grandchildren. In his spirit, he felt one step closer to reconciliation. He knew he had received God's forgiveness. He prayed he would receive his daughter's forgiveness.

He'd never imagined he would find his second chance at love in Spring Valley. When Ada started playing matchmaker at the coffee house, he remembered her saying she thought he and Alana would be the perfect match, and the Mockingbird Coffee House had proven to be a place of new beginnings. *Did he just have a Divine date?* he wondered. Had his Maker arranged a divine appointment with Alana or was it the self-appointed matchmaker? Alana was different than any other woman he'd ever been with, and she was also the only woman he'd ever dated that knew nothing of his world. He liked that she had no hidden agendas. On the drive back to the inn, he'd felt a sense of freedom after he'd shared the truth of his past with Alana. Upon first introductions, he'd always held the lingering fear that if someone knew the truth about him, they wouldn't accept him. He'd learned over time that revealing was the beginning of healing. He whispered to himself, *the truth will set you free*. Honesty always brought him freedom. Freedom to heal. Freedom to forgive. Freedom to love.

He had to remind himself that his alarm would sound in a few hours. He needed to go to bed since he had a full schedule ahead of him. He left the balcony and went back to his room. He slept in peace.

Chapter Twenty-Two

Organization was her superpower. Alana approached the Giving Tree wish granting project for the Haven House women's shelter like a professional gift concierge. She loved the idea of the Giving Tree and how it inspired a movement of generosity in Spring Valley. She loved that her nephew found his bride-to-be when Gabe and Shauna were teammates, chosen to sponsor a wishing ornament from the Giving Tree.

She loved shopping, leaving no stone unturned to find the perfect gift. So why did she feel nervous with her assignment? After all, reminding herself, her shopping partner was Santa Claus, the man who brings the gifts and places them under the tree.

It was a last-minute request for the wedding party to take on the wish granting project. She and Rich were assigned buying presents for the children. She'd created a holiday gift tracker spreadsheet with the child's name, age, gender, gift wish, and budget. She'd purchased kid's wrapping paper adorned with snowmen, candy canes, and reindeer as well as a dozen rolls of tape and colorful curling ribbon and bows. She'd set up a folding table in the corner of the kitchen as their wrapping station and scheduled Cydney to cover for her in the afternoon and evening. All she and Rich had to do was shop. By the end of the evening, they'd have everything wrapped, tagged, and delivered. At least, that was the plan.

***

It was too quick. The weekend passed in a blur. He'd spent every moment he could with Alana. They worked side-by-side—elf and Santa, at the last two pop-up cookie workshops. They took the Christmas Church Tour, strolled through Spring Valley where they visited churches in the downtown historic district, saw their beautifully decorated sanctuaries, enjoyed a handbells concert, sang carols, and sipped on cocoa. It wasn't an official date, but it felt like a date.

When he wasn't with her, he wished he was. Rich had his recovery meetings, his scheduled Santa appearances, and the Breakfast with Santa event. It was a sold-out crowd, but to his great disappointment, his grandchildren were a no-show. He couldn't help but worry that he'd missed his chance. He'd decided all he could do was wait and pray. He did both.

Rich dressed for their shopping date, came downstairs, and found Alana behind her desk in the lobby giving Cydney last minute instructions. He waited while the two stared at the computer screen discussing procedures.

"No worries. I've got this," Cydney assured

her.

"We don't have any late check-ins, so everything should be fine." Alana stood to leave. "If you have a problem, just give me a call on my cell."

That remark reminded him that he didn't have Alana's cell number. They were presently living under the same roof, but on many occasions, he had the overwhelming desire to call or text, but didn't have her number. He pulled out his phone and handed it to Alana.

"Would you put your contact information in my phone?"

She took the phone, but it was locked. She handed it back to him.

"You need to unlock it first."

He typed in 1225 and handed it back.

She'd been wanting to text him, but her *"strictly business"* declaration kept her from doing so. Since they'd been *fraternizing*, she would freely give him her number. She was taking their relationship to the next level. She promised herself she would try not to overload Rich with text messages. It would be difficult since he was always on her mind.

She grabbed the freshly-printed spreadsheet from the printer.

"Are you taking work with us?"

"It's our gift tracker spreadsheet."

Laying his finger aside of his nose, Rich confided in his Santa voice, "I normally use a scroll." He grinned and winked.

"We have to purchase gifts for eight children, and we only have a few hours to shop, wrap, and deliver. My spreadsheet will be a life saver."

"Let's go make some wishes come true."

He helped her with her coat and held the door open. As she passed, he whispered, "You're beautiful."

His gentle touch on her back sent a warm sensation through her body. He took her hand as they walked together, side-by-side. Sweet, she thought, he was perfect.

Three hours later they were back at the inn loaded down with shopping bags moving on to stage two of the evening—wrapping.

She loved holiday music and immediately opened her Spotify app and chose the Christmas Classics playlist. Since he'd memorized every word to every popular holiday song, she decided she couldn't go wrong with her choice. They began wrapping to the sounds of "Blue Christmas" by Elvis Presley.

"Did I ever tell you my mom almost named me Elvis?"

"No, but I can't imagine that I would have ever dated a guy named Elvis. I'm glad she went with Rich."

In his best impersonation he replied, "Thank you, thank you very much."

"You're good at those Southern accents." Irresistibly good, she thought. "How did you end up with the name Rich?"

"Mom was a huge fan of the King of Rock and Roll and pushed for Elvis, but dad was a huge fan of Richard Petty and —"

She interrupted, "Who's Richard Petty? Wasn't he a rocker?"

"No, you're thinking of the rocker, Tom Petty and the Heartbreakers. Richard Petty is a stock racing driver legend." He kept forgetting she knew nothing about his beloved sport. "He's nicknamed, 'The King.'"

"I've got a lot to learn."

"Yes, you do. I'm thinking mom and dad compromised since Elvis and Richard were both considered kings." He paused for a moment. "If you like, you can call me King."

Alana rolled her eyes and smiled. "I'll stick with Rich or Richard Ramsey if I want to be formal." She smiled.

Rich learned she took her job, any job, seriously as he watched her wrapping packages, moving fast.

"You could get a part-time gig as Santa's little helper wrapping presents at the mall. By the way, that reminds me, where's your elf outfit? I was looking forward to you wearing it tonight." He quickly raised his eyebrows up and down.

Her lips spread into a grin. "Only in your dreams." She tossed a roll of wrapping paper to him and instructed, "Get to work."

He slowed her project, walking to her side

of the table and inviting her into a slow, warm, gratifying kiss. When he heard voices outside the kitchen door, he eased back. "I've been wanting to do that all evening."

"What took you so long?" He made her weak. She wrapped her arms around his neck and gave him a more satisfying kiss. She pulled away and then leaned toward him again to rub her lips over his.

Slowly, she pushed him back to his side of the table. "If we keep this up, we'll never get this project finished."

Reluctantly, he complied.

He was really awful at gift wrapping. He'd never conquered that Christmassy skill. After a few minutes, frustration with the tape dispenser grew to a boiling point. "Wouldn't it have been easier to have gift bags?"

"Of course, it would have been easier for us, but it would've also been easier for curious kids sneaking a peek at presents."

"Oh, that's half the fun!"

"I'm shocked! You, of all people!"

"If they really want to know what's inside, kids are capable of unwrapping and rewrapping packages. It's part of the excitement." He confessed, "I may have been a little curious from time-to-time and took a peek. There's always going to be Present Peekers."

She doubled up the tape on her last gift. "This one is peeker-proofed." She added it to the stack of presents. "I think we're ready." She'd followed directions and had black trash bags ready to conceal the presents. She reached for a bag and started placing the gifts inside.

"Let's load these up in the truck."

Rich returned after his first trip. "Get your gloves. The temperature's dropped, and it's starting to snow."

Chapter Twenty-Three

Ada arranged to meet Rich and Alana at Haven House. She'd never involved herself in the wish granting from the Giving Tree because she'd always served as host and facilitator. It was up to the volunteers to adopt a wishing ornament and recruit others to fulfill the wish. But this wish, benefiting the women's rescue ministry, was different—it was a part of her. It was a Spirit-led idea that began as a seed planted in her heart and grew to a thriving ministry. As a believer, Ada felt God called us to live out our faith at home, at work, and in the community. She'd been a pastor's wife for over forty years and learned, via the school of hard knocks, how ministries succeed. She'd given up trying to do big things on her own when she found herself discouraged, defeated, and alone in her endeavors. She decided if the Spirit empowered the early church to turn the world upside down, He could equip her and an army of volunteers to make a difference in their community. She'd let the Spirit lead.

Before the shelter opened, she and J.R. had offered their home to defenseless women and children who were victims of domestic violence. The newly formed shelter was a testament to a Spirit-led, Spirit-empowered ministry. She believed every woman and child deserved shelter and a Merry Christmas, and she wanted to play a part in making their Christmas wishes happen.

She stood watch at the door for Santa's helpers. She saw the truck pass and park down the road in an empty spot.

Rich hoisted a bag over his shoulder. Since the day she'd learned his secret, Alana couldn't keep from teasing him about his part-time gig. "Carrying a bag over your shoulder has become second nature for you, hasn't it?"

He cocked his head and looked her in the eyes. "I'm beginning to regret telling you my secret."

"Are you kidding me? That made my Christmas!"

Ada watched the couple walking on the sidewalk. She thought if a passerby observed them smiling and engaged in conversation, they'd assume they were a long-term, happily married couple, embracing the joys of life. She had a sneaking suspicion her second attempt at matchmaking was on its way to becoming a splendid success. Joy danced in her heart.

Giddy, she opened the door before they knocked. "Get in here before you freeze. The snow is coming down harder."

They stood in the entryway waiting for Ada

to close the door and give directions.

She pointed to an open door. "Let's put them in the director's office, for now. She can keep them under lock and key until Christmas Eve." She took one of the bags from Alana and led the way. "I'll give you a quick tour after we stash these."

They tucked the bags in the corner of the office, and Ada led them to the original parlor, all decked out for the season.

"It's awfully quiet in here." Rich heard faint sounds coming from the other end of the house.

"They are on an outing to the mall. Otherwise, it would be very noisy this time of night."

"I see the rest of our crew has been busy." Alana loved the decorations.

"Yes, Colleen donated all the decorations from the Old Towne Christmas shop, and the rest of the clan spent an evening decorating."

Alana let her know, "Gabe is going to drop off the cookie decorating kits tomorrow afternoon. The kids will love them! They were a big hit at the workshops."

Rich was drawn to the scripture decoration on the wall: *God's safe-house for the battered, a sanctuary during bad times.* He'd met individuals in his recovery group that also found themselves in domestic abuse situations, living in a shelter. It was one thing listening to a story, he thought, but it's another seeing it in person. He felt the need to offer his assistance.

"Ada, are there any special projects you need funded?"

"As a matter of fact, there is. I just met with the director this week, and the number one need is transportation. Most of the women are fleeing a bad situation and don't have access to a car. We started a car donation program, and a couple of cars have been donated, but they are in need of repairs."

"You're talking my language. You can consider it done." His mind flipped from one mechanic to another that he would contact.

Ada looked heavenward. "Thank you, Jesus!"

"I'll call you in January and make arrangements. I already have a few people in mind that would be more than willing to volunteer. I'll make this an ongoing project," he promised.

Ada's jubilant spirit tickled Alana. Raised in New England, she was more reserved on matters of faith. She found it refreshing not only listening to Ada's praises to her Lord, but also Rich freely sharing his faith and its influence in his life. It was as natural as talking about the weather. They inspired her to examine her own journey of faith.

Ada heard the van pull into the driveway. "Since the snow is coming down, I'm going to go and help them haul things in." Before they could volunteer, she added, "Strangers make the residents a little uncomfortable, so you two mosey on along, and I'll see you later." She opened the door for a quick exit.

They didn't mosey. The snow made them scurry down the sidewalk to his truck. Rich, always the gentleman, held the door open for Alana. As he walked to the other side of the truck, that's when he saw them. His daughter and grandchildren were getting out of the van. He was stunned.

He got in the truck. Alana didn't know what it was, but in a few seconds, he went from joyful to troubled. "Are you okay?"

The truck was facing the other direction, so he was sure Courtney didn't see him. Plus, she was busy helping the kids get into the shelter. It felt like a knife to his heart. He held his chest. He could barely breathe.

"Rich, you're starting to scare me." She unbelted her seat belt to scoot closer.

He looked at her as his eyes welled up. "Just give me a minute. Would you call Ada and ask her to meet us at the coffee house?"

"I will, but I'm pretty sure it's closed."

"That's even better. We'll have some privacy." He put the truck in gear and headed to the coffee house.

It wasn't easy for Alana to keep her mouth shut. It wasn't a request; she just had the feeling he needed to process whatever happened and didn't need interrogated. The questions that swirled around in her mind would be answered at the coffee house. He reached over and held her hand. She could feel his strong pulse throbbing in his wrist. She worried.

They pulled into the parking lot of the old church building. He'd calmed. Rich always felt like he was going to church when he stopped in for coffee. It had a way of setting his heart and mind in a good place. He needed to be in a good place. Ada was known as the local problem solver and prayer warrior. He needed both.

Rich didn't mind the silence. He was accustomed to being alone. Yet he had to consider the woman sitting next to him, wondering what she thought of him and his distant, far-away mood.

"I know it just took a couple of minutes to drive here. I'm sorry I clammed up, and thank you for not bombarding me with questions."

She'd waited patiently but asked a second time, "Are you okay? Do we need to go to the emergency room?"

"I'm not okay, but it's not my heart health. It's my broken heart. I'm troubled. I'm happy. Distraught. Confused." He wiped his eyes with his glove. "When we were leaving, I saw Courtney and the kids getting out of the van." His spirit was crushed with the weight of the reality. "My family is living in a shelter for abused women and children. I don't know what to do, and I'm hoping Ada can help."

The beam from Ada's car headlights swept through the cab of the truck, revealing the distraught couple. Ada whispered, "Lord, give me the words."

They got out of the truck, then Alana walked to Rich and embraced him before they entered the coffee house. Ada locked the door behind them, made sure the closed sign was posted, and switched on a light.

"I came as quick as I could. What's happened?" She gestured toward a booth for them to have a seat and scooted into the bench across the table.

"I don't know how else to say this, but to just come right out and ask." Rich was anxious. "I just saw my daughter and grandchildren getting out of the van and going into the shelter house. Did you know they were my relatives?"

Ada didn't appreciate the accusatory tone but knew he was hurting. "Rich, I had no idea."

Alana, surprised by his tone, reminded him, "How would she have known? You said you didn't even know Courtney's last name until you saw the sign-up sheet for the Santa Breakfast."

Embarrassment stirred in him. He put his elbows on the table and rested his head in his hands, rubbing his temples. "I'm sorry, Ada. I'm just overwhelmed right now. Can you tell me anything?"

"Rich, I know very little details about the residents. For their safety, it's strictly confidential. But even if I knew, I couldn't disclose any information. I'm sure you can understand the circumstance."

He nodded in agreement. He knew in his mind, but his heart only wanted answers.

"Is there anything you could do? Anything?" He'd beg on knees if needed.

Ada leaned back and stared off in space for a few seconds waiting for divine intervention.

It came.

"Since it's Christmas, is there anything personal she would recognize that you could gift? I know it's been a long time, but maybe something from her childhood?"

He leaned back with his hands behind his head and breathed a sigh of relief. "Ada, I could kiss you right now!"

"Save your kisses for Alana, just tell me your idea."

"I have a stuffed teddy bear from her childhood that was her best friend. It's all love-worn. She dragged that bear everywhere. It never left her side. She named him, Teddy." Rich had a glimmer of hope.

"You could write a short little note, attached to the stuffed bear, in a wrapped gift. I will ask the director to place it under the tree. Then you'll just have to wait and let her make the next move." She leaned in, making sure she had his attention, and he heard every word. "Rich, you have to be prepared; she may choose to not respond." Ada had to consider Courtney's feelings over her father's. "Neither of you can reveal Courtney's whereabouts. She's there for her and her children's safety. But first, before you do anything, I have to clear this with the director. I'll call her in the morning." Ada grabbed a napkin and dug a pen out of her purse for Rich to write his phone number. "Give me your number, and I'll let you know if the director gives us the go-ahead."

Ada was a hugger, and she hugged them both goodbye.

As the couple left the coffee shop, Ada locked the door behind them. Before they reached the truck, they heard her say, "God bless you two!"

Rich felt blessed.

Chapter Twenty-Four

Rich and Alana dashed back to the inn. He wanted to write the note and get Teddy wrapped, even before he had the official go-ahead from the director. Alana started organizing and packing away their gift-wrapping workstation in the kitchen. She sat aside the perfect box and paper.

Rich found Teddy right where he left him on the fireplace mantle. He picked Teddy up and looked the stuffed bear straight in the eye and talked to him like an old friend. "I promised that someday I would reunite you with your girl. I'm keeping my promise."

He'd always kept a stash of Christmas cards handy. He pulled one out, said a quick prayer, wrote Courtney a short note, and sealed the envelope. He went downstairs to prepare Teddy for his trip.

He found Alana packing away the supplies. Two Diet Cokes were on the countertop.

"Help yourself, and if you don't mind, pour mine in a glass."

Rich carefully sat Teddy on the worktable and retrieved the drinks.

She stacked up the last plastic container and sipped her soda.

"When you showed me your red suit, I saw the stuffed bear in your room and wondered what this little guy was all about."

"Teddy is all about love and hope." He sat down, emotionally drained. "Thank you for using your wicked wrapping skills for this last gift."

"It's my pleasure." She skillfully wrapped his gift of hope and handed it to him.

"You look exhausted," she said sweetly.

"I am. Would you hate me if I call it a night?" He stood and scooted the chair under the table.

"I could never hate you." She hugged him and nuzzled against his chest.

He kissed her gently on her forehead. "Thank you for understanding. I'll see you tomorrow."

With the gift tucked under his arm, he headed up the back stairway to his room. He'd hoped he could sleep, but he had so much on his mind.

Chapter Twenty-Five

S hortly before nine the following morning, the text from Ada brought an end to his anxiousness. The director would allow the gift, but only if Ada delivered the package, and Rich would no longer be allowed to enter the shelter. He could drop the package off at the coffee house before closing.

He sent Alana his first text.

Rich: *We've been given the green light! Operation Return Teddy is a go! Can we meet at the coffee house at 7?*

He grinned when her response arrived almost instantly.

Alana: *Fantastic! I'll meet you there.* ❤

Rich dressed in his red suit for a morning drop-in visit at the nursing home. The self-proclaimed over-fifty-and-fit club member had been transformed into the jolly old elf, who shook when he laughed like a bowl full of jelly.

He stood in front of the mirror, cinching his belt. When Santa Claus came to town, he reminisced, finding love was not on his schedule. He'd never imagined a chance encounter would link his lonely heart with Alana's and give him a glimmer of hope for a promising Christmas. To think that he might also reunite with his daughter was almost too much to imagine. Then he reminded himself, *God can do anything, you know— far more than you could ever imagine!* He smiled.

***

It was after seven when Rich and Alana entered the coffee house with his special delivery package. The final phase of Operation Return Teddy was underway. They made their way to the counter to place their drink order. The wonderful aromas of vanilla, cinnamon, and spice coffee were so thick, you could almost cut the ambiance with a knife.

"I feel like celebrating." Rich eyed the dessert menu board. "Let's have a slice of Ada's signature Hummingbird cake."

"You go ahead. I'll just have coffee since I'm still on my sugar detox." Eyeing the cake in the bakery display, she frowned. "I'm counting down the days until this sugar fast ends on Christmas Day. Did you know Gabe and Shauna chose the Hummingbird recipe for their wedding cake?"

"That's an unusual choice."

"It's part of their love story. Everything in their wedding is symbolic." She paused and ordered her low calorie, low sugar Gingerbread Latte. "Their wedding is so romantic."

From the kitchen serving window, Ada saw the couple. "I reserved you a booth in the balcony. I'll join you in a couple of minutes." She'd selected her favorite matchmaking booth, tucked in the corner for privacy.

They climbed the steps of the grand entrance stairway. The banister draped with festive green winter garland and carols playing in the background served as the perfect setting for a special Christmas mission. They found their reserved table.

They sat their package, drinks, and cake on the table. Starting to unbundle, Rich helped Alana with her jacket. Always the gentleman, she thought. She'd grown accustomed to this gesture.

Rich also shed his coat, carefully hanging both on the coat hangers attached to the vintage style wooden booth. He chose to sit across from her, so he could focus on her beautiful face.

Rich took his first bite of cake. "This is heavenly. You have to try it."

Alana shook her head. "No, don't tempt me."

"It's basically a basket of fruit. It's chuck-full of bananas, pineapple, and pecans." He smiled, filled his fork, and reached over to tempt her.

"You left out cream cheese, butter, and sugar." How could she resist the temptation? She asked herself, *How could she resist him?* She took a bite and closed her eyes, savoring each morsel. "It's sweet, fruity, and spicy. It's a tropical vacation in my mouth."

"It's intoxicating, is what it is." He indulged in a few more bites.

Two festive trees stood proudly in the

opposite corner of the balcony. The Giving Tree, a program granting wishes for a community member in need, was decorated with ornaments. The little scrolls, originally attached to the ornament that held the written requests had all been distributed, and volunteers were making wishes come true. The Memory Tree, Ada's most recent program, was adorned with pictures and memorabilia to honor and mourn lives lost during the pandemic. Ada was determined they would not be forgotten.

"Gabe placed an ornament on the Memory Tree, honoring Mr. Barkley, who lived across the street from the inn." Alana pointed toward the tree. "They considered Gabe their guardian angel."

"Ada's a special lady. She's always thinking of others." Somberly he gazed at the tree remembering those he knew that didn't survive the pandemic.

"I wasn't able to attend the lighting of the Memory Tree last week. Gabe said it was standing room only. J.R. held a brief Celebration of Life service and talked of the legacy they left behind."

From the balcony, Rich could see the scripture plaque over the door that read, *The Lord bless thee, and keep thee,* reminding him of his conversation with Ada. "When I was talking to Ada a few weeks ago, she said this coffee house was her divine calling. She's a town treasure."

"Here she comes now." Alana spied Ada greeting customers as she made her way to their booth.

"You look a lot better tonight than you did last night," Ada surmised, seeing hope beaming from his eyes.

"I'm sorry if I came across as accusatory. I beg your forgiveness."

"No need to beg. I forgave you last night."

She patted the box. "So, this is Teddy?"

"I know he'll be in good hands. There's a 'Do Not Open Until Christmas' sticker on top. So, we'll see what happens."

"Wait and pray is my advice," Ada encouraged him.

"I've been hearing that a lot lately."

"Ada, we were admiring the Memory Tree. What a wonderful gesture. You are such a blessing." Alana surprised herself using a religious Southern phrase. She thought Ada and Rich were rubbing off on her. She added, "I've only lived here for two years, but I've learned that Spring Valley is a better place because of you and your acts of kindness."

Rich's heart flipped to hear Alana openly and honestly share her feelings.

Ada's eyes misted. Whatever she'd done, she didn't do for praise from man. She'd always tried to find ways to reveal and give God's love. But if she were honest, and she always tried to be, even with herself, it felt good to hear words of appreciation. "Thank you, so much. That's such a sweet thing to say." Ada stood with the package in hand. "I better get back downstairs. It's always chaotic near closing time."

Rich stood and gave Ada a bear hug and whispered in her ear, "God bless you, you sweet angel."

Ada prayed over Teddy as she carried the gift of hope downstairs.

They left the coffee shop hand-in-hand and walked the short distance back in casual conversation. Rich held the kitchen door open for Alana where they found Jean and a man laughing and chatting in the kitchen.

"Look, Alana, you have a visitor!" Jean announced.

Rich stood in the doorway as a stranger turned, quickly made his way to Alana, picked her up, twirled her around, and finished his greeting with a passionate kiss. From Rich's vantage point, he'd thought the way she responded, this man in her kitchen was certainly no stranger. After the man let her feet touch the floor, he held the embrace until she gently broke away remembering to introduce Rich.

Trying to catch her breath and gain her composure, she put her hand lightly on the man's back and made formal introductions. "Let me introduce you to Rich." Pausing for a millisecond, she didn't know what came over her and also didn't know what to call Rich. "This is Rich Ramsey, a guest at the inn." She looked away from Rich. "Rich, this is Everett Davenport, from

Asheville."

Of course, his name was Everett, he'd thought. From the navy blazer, polo shirt, chinos, and cashmere scarf around his neck, he screamed preppy dude. Sawyer, Preston, Carter, Everett—any choice would not have surprised Rich.

Everett wrapped his arm around Alana's waist, claiming his territory.

Challenged, Rich lacked the emotional fortitude to contest and made the impulsive decision to retreat. He excused himself. Shocked and confused, his raw emotions led him upstairs to his room. Alone. His hopes crumbled.

Chapter Twenty-Six

H e tried not to live in the past. His holiday scheduled filled with appearances, holiday shopping, and time spent with Alana helped secret away his failures, at least during those hours his mind stayed occupied. After attending a recovery small group meeting, he'd returned to an empty house. Alone with his thoughts. He sat at the bar in his own entertainment room with a Diet Coke to quench his thirst and an open Bible for his soul.

Though disheartened and depressed, Rich prayed, thanking God for his recovery group and the hope in God's power. He'd kept alcohol at bay— it was the current heartache and guilt that tried to rob him of his sanity. He held fast to the scripture: *For it is God who works in you to will and act in order to fulfill his good purpose.*

He knew in his heart that God was working in his life. But today, he was brokenhearted.

He was a little angry, too. Had he misinterpreted Alana's attention? If he'd known she was involved with another man, he would have kept the door to his heart tightly closed.

He thought it could just be him

overreacting. It could be just an old acquaintance dropping in unannounced, bringing Alana and Jean holiday greetings.

It could be, he decided, he'd been a fool.

He considered remaining at the inn, but he knew he couldn't avoid her. He still had obligations in Spring Valley, but now, at least, they wouldn't be under the same roof. He'd convinced himself leaving was the best decision—*or would it be the worst?*

Deep down, he knew he'd handled it wrong.

He glanced at the awards, trophies, and sports memorabilia that lined his bookcase. He'd always jokingly called it the 'look how great I am' wall. He'd taken pride in his communication skills. Good communication was critical between the crew chief and his driver. He'd spent his career constantly communicating with his driver, talking pit strategies or just trying to calm his driver down after a disastrous bump and run.

He scolded himself. *Why did he fail so miserably communicating with Alana? What was he thinking when he left without explanation?* He didn't feel so great now.

He'd had nerves of steel atop the pit box making quick decisions. Rich knew the odds. Every week only one crew chief took a win. Every race, a single decision could determine a victory. He was watched by millions of people, his decisions scrutinized and second guessed at every turn. He wasn't afraid of making calls. He'd had to in order to succeed. Even if it were the wrong call and his last call. *Why was he letting fear control his decisions now?* He knew the answer. He didn't care how millions felt about him. He only cared what Alana felt. She'd won over his heart; he didn't want to lose her—he feared he had.

He was determined to move forward in God's grace. In his sadness, hope shown through when he spotted the empty space on the bookcase where Teddy once sat. He kept his promise to Teddy—he'd found his girl. He reminded himself he was one step closer to reuniting with his daughter—making repairs. One step closer to getting to know his grandchildren—being called Papaw.

From the moment he'd walked into the women's shelter carrying a load of presents for strangers' children to discovering his daughter and grandchildren were homeless and escaping domestic abuse, Rich had conflicting feelings of guilt and goodness.

The personal guilt. The guilt that lived in the shadows. Owning responsibility of his past failures. If he'd been sober, he considered, Courtney may have never left home. He also felt the overwhelming goodness of God's promises. The scripture entered his thoughts: *Let us hold unswervingly to the hope we profess, for he who promised is faithful.*

He wept.

The success of his personal recovery journey

relied on the promises of God, where he'd found freedom from his past and hope for his future. Hope, love, and promises fulfilled were the greatest gifts he could have ever imagined.

When he'd laid the Bible on the counter, it opened to the psalmist. He began reading. *Why, my soul, are you downcast? Why so disturbed within me? Put your hope in God, for I will yet praise Him, my Savior and my God.*

He resolved, with or without Alana, he had to continue moving forward in faith.

Chapter Twenty-Seven

For the next few days, Alana occupied her mind with assisting Jean with last minute wedding tasks. Additional rooms at the inn were booked for out-of-town guests, and transportation was set for to-and-from the venue. Boutonnieres and corsages were ordered for the immediate family, and of course, Gabe requested his mom's award-winning cookies in place of a groom's cake. She'd not been Chef Jean's choice for assisting with baking, but Jean was desperate.

She loved that the couple chose a rustic wedding theme, incorporating all the elements that brought the two love birds together.

Alana had a backflash to her lavish wedding with Daniel Davis. Actually, she corrected herself, it was more of her mother's wedding than her own. Her mother thought it was Boston's social event of the year. Alana felt like it was more of a merger between multi-millionaire families. It was an opulent affair with the picturesque harbor as a backdrop, complete with an orchestra and real silver place settings. Guests went away impressed, but all the glitz and glamour slowly faded. Her groom broke his vows, and the merger ended when she'd signed divorce papers.

She'd thought a second chance looked promising with Rich. Maybe, she considered, she'd sabotaged her happily ever after.

By the time she'd finished her to-do list, it was almost midnight. She knocked on her sister's door. She needed sister-to-sister talk therapy. She heard Jean's permission to enter. She found her sister modeling her dress for the wedding.

"You look amazing."

Alana was impressed with the red stylish three-piece ensemble, embellished with beading on the top, jacket, and pant. She'd grown accustomed to only seeing Jean in her chef uniforms, and she was beautiful in her wedding attire.

"Thank you! I've been lounging around in luxury tonight. I wanted to give it a trial run. It's very comfortable."

"And it's not black!"

"Smarty pants. I happen to love black, but the bride and groom asked that I match the bridal party's Christmassy colors."

Jean spun a playful twirl. "It's even ideal for dancing."

"So, you'll be dancing?"

"That's my plan. What's kept you up so late? Wait, let me guess. You want to talk about your love life." She raised one eyebrow. "I wish you would get this settled one way or another before the wedding. We don't need all this drama."

"Well, excuse me, I don't need it either."

Jean plopped down on the bed in her fancy garb and patted the bed, expecting her sister to sit. Instead, Alana fell backwards emotionally exhausted.

"Have you heard from Rich?"

"No, not a word. Not even a text."

"Have you contacted him?"

Alana shook her head no.

"You want to tell me why not? From our last conversation, you slammed the door on reuniting with your ex, Everett, because you were in love with Rich."

"Correction, I didn't say love."

"It may not have been spoken, but it was definitely implied." She scolded Alana. "What did you expect Rich to think? That passionate, lingering kiss Everett gave you would have shocked anyone."

"It didn't mean anything; my response was muscle memory. Everett always had a way of taking my breath away."

"Everett knew you were on a date, and as soon as you walked through that door, he let everyone know he was reclaiming his territory. I thought if you didn't realize he was still a jerk, you would've with that ridiculous move."

Alana knew she didn't have the best track record with choosing men. "I'm sure women envied me because of my handsome surgeon husband. But I kept Daniel's infidelities secret. We were raised Catholic, and I believed in marriage. I believed in forgiveness and second chances."

"You went beyond second chances with him. You gave Daniel second, third, and fourth chances. He even cheated on you before you married. If that didn't qualify for a Catholic annulment, I don't know what would."

"That's why we divorced. And then Everett, Mr. Noncommittal Everett, entered my life and basically wasted my time. I finally met the man of my dreams with Rich, and I blew it." Alana pulled herself upright and sat crossed leg. "Am I falling in love with Santa?"

"No, my dear, you've fallen in love with Rich Ramsey. Why did you let him go?"

"I didn't let him go; he just left. I'm afraid I've lost him."

Jean could see the same heartbroken look her sister had as a teenager, sitting on her bed, talking through tears.

"What do you think I should do?"

Offering sisterly advice, Jean suggested, "The first thing in the morning, you should take a drive out into the country and find the man you think you lost."

"I think you're right." Alana agreed.

"I know I'm right."

Chapter Twenty-Eight

E arly Christmas eve, the director of Haven House asked Courtney to join her and Ada in the office. She handed her a wrapped gift. "Courtney, this is highly unusual, but Ada and I discussed the situation, and we think you should open your gift this morning while the kids are busy decorating cookies."

Courtney took the unexpected gift, baffled by why the director thought she needed privacy.

"We'll give you a few minutes. If you need to talk, we'll be in the parlor."

Courtney sat on the couch and began opening the meticulously wrapped package. She lifted the lid from the box and saw her love-worn childhood toy. She blinked away the tears that welled up. She held him close as cherished memories of Christmases past filled her heart. Her father's laughter. Her mother's dancing to holiday music. Unwrapping gifts under the tree. The memories of a child loved. The memories before she lost her mother.

She opened the card and read the note: *Courtney, it's your dad. Miracles happen. I met my grandchildren. I'm the Spring Valley Santa. When I saw you that day at the Train Depot, I didn't reveal my identity because it wasn't the right timing. I just want you to know, I'm not the dad you knew when you left home. I became a changed man when I turned my life over to Christ. I'm twenty years sober. Your grandparents' home is available if you and the kids want to move in and live temporarily or permanently. It's yours. There are no strings attached—None. I love you. You can call me at any time, day or night. Love, Dad*

Tears stained the note.

Courtney looked in his eyes and talked to her old friend, "Teddy, what do you think about Santa?" It might have been her imagination, but she'd swear his eyes twinkled.

She opened the door and asked if she could talk with Ada.

Chapter Twenty-Nine

A lana sat staring from the window of her car. She shivered, not from the snowy scene that welcomed her, but from her strong emotions and the surge of adrenaline that rushed through her body triggering a fight-or-flight response. Fear of rejection screamed, *FLEE*. Her heart whispered, *fight*. She needed to fight for her love with Rich—a love she felt was worth the bruises on both of their hearts.

His house and yard reflected the spirit of the season decorated in the best holiday décor. She smiled, thinking she wouldn't expect anything less for the man who embodied the spirit of Christmas. The snow lightly falling on the yard ornaments added a sweet charm to the shabby plastic Santa with a bag of toys slung over his back. She'd tried to picture in her mind the blow-mold lawn ornament when Rich shared the story. He'd not fully explained the sparking twinkle in its eye. The twinkle that should have faded over time but still glistened. The twinkling-eyed Santa that gave Rich and his family so much joy.

Finding time for love was not on her holiday calendar, she reminded herself, and falling in love so quickly and easily was definitely not in her plans. But Rich had entered her heart, and there he would stay. She opened the car door, and the fear that clawed through her almost stopped her from getting out of the car, from taking the next step. But she'd learned from Rich to step out in faith. Snowflakes drifted and swirled around her. Doubt and hope accompanied her to his front porch. She took a deep breath and pushed the doorbell button.

She waited. He didn't answer the door.

The sound of his truck echoed down the long driveway. She turned and saw him returning home. He saw her standing at the door. He pushed his foot harder on the gas pedal. Excitement raced through him. She walked toward the moving vehicle, anticipating where he might stop. Before he could get out of the truck, she opened the passenger door and jumped inside. He slid the shifter into neutral, set the emergency brake, and kept the engine running to warm the cab. His old truck, Betsy, was part of his family story. His restoration of Betsy was all about restoring metal and memories. Looking at the woman who sat across from him, he wondered what story he'd add today. He hoped it was a story of restoration.

"Fancy meeting you here." He was first to break the ice.

"When no one answered, I was afraid I wouldn't get to see you before the wedding, and I wanted to talk to you in person."

His throat tightened. That phrase was

usually followed by the 'It's not you, it's me' farewell speech. With his eyes on her, he braced himself.

"I need you to know that I asked Everett to leave the night he showed up at the inn." She swallowed hard. "Everett and I dated on and off for years, but I broke it off before moving to Spring Valley. He showed up, uninvited, wanting to rekindle our relationship. He caught me off guard."

Rich thought she wasn't the only one caught off guard. He let her talk.

"He was a jerk for the way he acted in front of you. I told him I had no feelings for him, and he needed to leave. I didn't know you had left until Cydney went to clean your room, and you were gone."

"I left a note to charge me for the remaining dates I had booked."

"I saw your note. Do you think I was worried about losing out on a room charge? The only thing I was afraid of was losing you forever. I'm in love with you, Richard Ramsey."

He'd waited to hear those words—healing words to his wounded heart.

"Alana—"

"No, let me finish. I don't know how or when it happened. Maybe it was love at first sight when you walked into the lobby and introduced yourself. I don't know, but I do know I've fallen in love with you. I can't imagine spending Christmas without you, or New Year's or any other day. I want you in my life for the rest of my life." She studied his eyes, waiting for a response.

She was shocked to see him open his truck door and step out. She'd feared he retreated as he did the night he left the inn. He walked to the passenger side, opened the door, and took her by the arm. "It's too crowded in there to do this." He drew her to him, and his lips crushed down on hers. "I love you, Alana, and I promise you all my Christmases for the rest of my life."

In response, she wrapped her arms around his neck and pulled him in for another passionate kiss. They paid no attention to the steady fall of snow—until his cell phone rang.

He opened the door for Alana to get back into the warm cab of his truck.

He looked at the screen. "I think this may be Courtney." He answered the phone and motioned for Alana to slide over, so he could join her in the truck. He was quiet. The person on the other end carried the conversation. He remained silent and listened. Alana's heart thumped in her chest.

"I understand, whatever is best for you and the kids." A long pause was followed by, "Goodbye."

He put his head in his hands and wept uncontrollably. Tears carrying all the years of remorseful guilt and pain stained his palms. Alana wrapped comforting arms around him. He held her and whispered through his tears. "She's coming home! They're coming home!"

Chapter Thirty

Proudly officiating the wedding, Ada directed, "Gabe, please take Shauna's hand and repeat after me: Shauna, from this day forward, I promise to walk by your side forever. I promise to help you and encourage you in all that you do. I promise to love you forever."

Hand in hand, Rich and Alana sat together in the audience witnessing the Christmas Day wedding and sacred vows. Rich leaned in close and whispered in her ear, "I promise to love you forever."

THE END

Scripture Reference

Scripture Reference

"He heals the brokenhearted and bind
up their wounds." Psalm 177:3

"The Lord Bless thee and keep thee."
Numbers 6:24

"God's safe-house for the battered, a
sanctuary during bad times."
Psalm 9:9 (The Message)

"Don't worry about anything; instead
pray about everything."
Philippians 4:6

"What is your life? For you are a mist that
appears for a little time, then vanishes."
James 4:14

"That at the name of Jesus every knee should bow."
Philippians 2:10

"For you have been my hope, Lord, my
confidence since my youth."
Psalm 71:5

"Whom not having known you love; in whom, though now you don't see him, yet believing, you rejoice greatly with joy unspeakable and full of glory."
I Peter 1:8

"What a beautiful thing, God, to give thanks, to sing an anthem to you."
Psalm 92:1

"Again, Jesus spoke to them saying, 'I am the light of the world, whoever follows me will not walk in darkness, but will have the light of life.'"
John 8:12

"Then you will know the truth, and the truth will set you free."
John 8:32

"For it is God who works in you to will and act in order to fulfill his good purpose."
Philippians 2:13

"God can do anything, you know—far more than you could ever imagine!"
Ephesians 3:20 (The Message)

"Let us hold unswervingly to the hope we profess, for he who promised is faithful."
Hebrews 10:23

"Why, my soul, are you downcast? Why so disturbed within me? Put your hope in God, for I will yet praise him, my Savior and my God."

Psalm 42:5

*Serenity Prayer Credits
Reinhold Niebuhr*

*PRAYER FOR SERENITY
God, grant me the serenity
to accept the things I cannot change,
the courage to change the things I can,
and the wisdom to know the difference.
Living one day at a time,
enjoying one moment at a time;
accepting hardship as a pathway to peace;
talk, as Jesus did,
this sinful world as it is,
not as I would have it;
trusting that You will make all things right
if I surrender to Your will;
so that I may be reasonably happy in this life
and supremely happy with You forever in the next.
Amen.*

Celebrate Recovery is a Christ-centered, 12 step recovery program for anyone struggling with hurt, pain or addiction of any kind.
www.celebraterecovery.com

The mission of 58:12 Rescue is to provide a

safe Christ-centered home for vulnerable women and children that have been devastated by sexual abuse and/or domestic violence.

www.5812global.org

A portion of proceeds from *Santa's Promising Christmas* will be donated to 58:12 Global.

About the Author

A Note from Georgia

A big heartfelt thank you for reading *Santa's Promising Christmas*! I hope you enjoyed Rich and Alana's story and found it to be an inspirational love story that illustrates how relying on God's everlasting promises offers peace, love, and hope in an unended world. I pray for God's special Christmas blessing on you and yours.

If you did enjoy *Santa's Promising Christmas*, I would love for you to write a review. Reviews are a huge help to authors and I would love to read your feedback, and it's a great help for readers interested in one of my books for the first time.

You can post a review on Amazon or go to my website and leave a review message, sign up for New Releases in 2023, Blog Posts, and Giveaways: www.georgiacurtisling.com

If you haven't read *The Ornament of Hope*, book one in the Spring Valley Series, be sure to check it out and see where it all began. You'll love it!

Thank you and Christmas blessings!
Georgia

- Spring Valley Heartwarming Romance Series -
The Ornament of Hope
Santa's Promising Christmas

About the Author

Georgia Curtis Ling

Born and raised in the foothills of the Appalachian Mountains, Georgia holds dear the three inherent mountain values of faith, family, and the land. Her *Spring Valley Series*, including *The Ornament of Hope* and *Santa's Promising Christmas*, are rich with voices from the past, memories of heartwarming stories, and traditions of her cherished heritage. She and her husband, Phil, live in central Kentucky, just a few hours' drive from their son, Philip, and daughter-in-heart Lauren.

Georgia is the bestselling author of *What's in the Bible for Women, Mom's Lead in Love*, and *In Mom They Trust.* She touches the heart and tickles the funny bone as she writes about faith, love, and life. Over her career, her work has appeared in numerous periodicals and nine bestselling books.

For new release dates go to:
www.georgiacurtisling.com

Made in the USA
Monee, IL
08 December 2022

20126009R00127